The Sumerian Trinity

How Abraham discovered God in ancient Mesopotamia

Donna Berrot

Illustrations by Daniel Whettam

Copyright (c) 2004 Donna Berrot

All rights reserved. The use of any part of this publication, reproduced, transmitted in any form or by any means electronic, mechanical, photocopying, recording or otherwise, or store in a retrieval system without the prior written consent of the publisher is an infringement of the copyright law.

ISBN: 978-1-926633-48-0

Printed and bound in Hamilton, Ontario
Titles on Demand
www.titlesondemand.ca

Preface

Where did the God of Abraham and the stories about him in the Bible come from? These questions have been debated by scholars for more than a century, but the answers to these questions lie in the ruins of ancient Mesopotamia... present-day Iraq.

Clay tablets with remarkable resemblances to the Biblical Flood Story were discovered more than a hundred years ago in northern Iraq, and these discoveries showed clearly that the first chapters of the Bible were derived from Mesopotamian sources. But if the stories about God in the first eleven chapters of Genesis came from ancient Mesopotamia, how did this occur?

In this book the author proposes a theory as to how it could have happened. The scenes and conversations described in this book are conjectural, but they are based on a large body of historical and literary evidence. The reader is invited to imagine themselves in the countryside of Iraq 4000 years ago, looking back another 4000 years into the mists of time to see how it all began,

On a faraway day...

Contents

1. Journey to Nippur
2. The Land Beyond the River
3. The Story of Adam
4. The Rediscovery of Nippur
5. The Great Flood
6. The First Great Civilisation
7. The Story of the Tower
8. The Invention of Writing
9. The History of the Temple
10. The Call
11. Epilogue

Figure 1. Statuette of a Semitic man carrying a sacrificial lamb (ca. 1800 BC). Discovered in the ancient city of Mari by André Parrot. Gypsum, Aleppo Museum, Syria; height 9 inches.

Chapter 1

Journey to Nippur

"Abe!" shouted his father, "Take a flock of sheep to the temple for the evening sacrifices."

Abram's father was one of the head shepherds over the animal pens of Drehem, where flocks and herds from all over the empire were prepared for their final journey to the great temple of En-lil, patron god of Nippur and 'Lord of the Four Quarters of the World.'

Drehem was less than ten miles from Nippur, but the animals could not be rushed or they would lose their condition. The journey took half the day, and after their arrival at the temple the animals had to be slaughtered, cleaned, washed and prepared in good time for the evening sacrifices, which must be offered just as the red globe of the sun dipped below the flat western horizon. This meant eating breakfast in the semi-darkness and leaving at sunrise, before the searing heat of the sun had warmed up the land.

Nippur was upstream from Drehem on the River Euphrates, often referred to in ancient times as the Great River. Just over fifty miles to the east was another great river, the Tigris, and between them, an almost-perfectly-flat plain that the Greeks would later call Mesopotamia, the 'Land between the Rivers.'

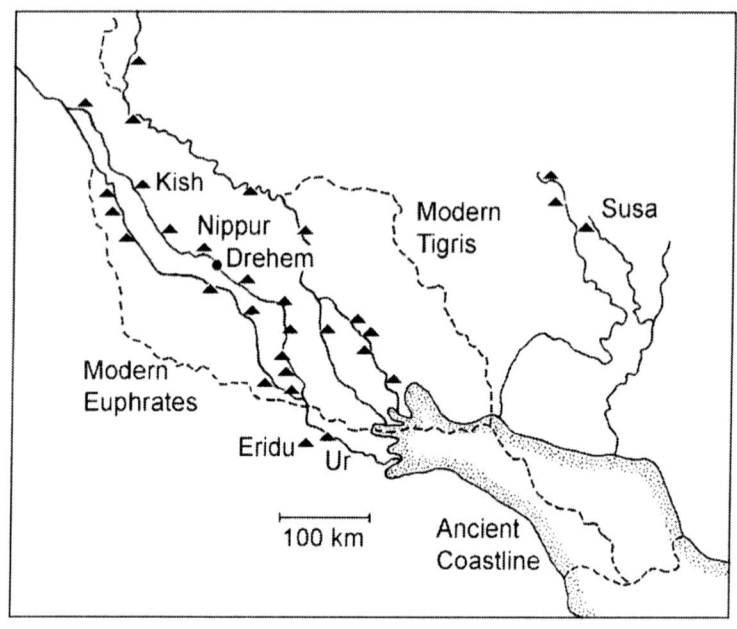

Figure 2. Map of Mesopotamia showing the locations of some important ancient cities relative to Drehem and the ancient courses of the Tigris and Euphrates. Dashed lines indicate the modern coastline and river courses.

Nippur was almost at the centre of the plain, and this had given it a strategic importance through much of Mesopotamian history. Indeed, for nearly 700 years before the birth of Abram,[1] Nippur had been the religious 'capital' of Mesopotamia, with the great temple of En-lil the focus of worship for the whole land.

Abram's family had not always lived at Drehem.[2] They were

---

[1] After he emigrated to the 'promised land' Abram was renamed Abraham as a sign of God's covenant.

[2] Drehem was also known as Puzrich-Dagan after the Semitic god Dagan, god of thunder.

descended from a long line of shepherds from northern Mesopotamia, where Abram's father was born on the wide rolling expanses of coarse grassland. But when Shulgi succeeded his father as king of Ur and ruler over all Mesopotamia in 2100 BC, he made Drehem the distribution centre for temple offerings from the whole empire.

Each province sent its tribute, either in cash or kind, but the different provinces had different products. The irrigated lands of the south produced grain, wine, fruit and dates, whereas the provinces of the northern steppes raised sheep and goats. These animals were all taken to Drehem before distribution to the great temples of the plain.

Abram's father had come down from the northern plains as a young man, bringing a flock of sheep raised by his father, but the work at Drehem was good, so he sent for his wife, settled down at Drehem, and raised a family there.

Figure 3. View of the northern plains near the ancient mound of Nimrud, with the River Tigris meandering into the distance.

The road from Drehem to Nippur followed the Euphrates, but was separated from the river by a wilderness of palm trees and shrubbery growing on the damp soil near the river bank. However, at intervals, irrigation canals cut through the wilderness, and in these places Abram could catch sight of the wide sweep of the river through gaps in the trees.

The river was the great trade route of the empire, and sometimes you could catch a glimpse between the trees of a barge, either being laboriously poled up river by the sweating crew or drifting downstream with the current.

Figure 4. A boat being poled along a river with vegetated banks. The horned hat of the central figure indicates his divinity. Impression of a 2300 BC cylinder seal, Musée du Louvre. Height 1 inch.

Sometimes, even more unusual craft could be seen on the river, the circular boats that brought cargoes down from the far north. On those upper reaches of the river, the current was so swift that the boats could not be paddled upstream, so the traders would make a boat from a wooden frame covered with hides. And on each of these boats there would be a group of donkeys; so that when they arrived at their destination, the men would unload their cargo, dismantle the boat, and load the skins on the donkeys to return to their homeland.

Most of the cities of the plain could be reached by river or canal, so barges were used for ceremonial journeys by high officials, and even by the gods. When this happened, the statue of the god would be carried down to the river on a kind of sedan chair, and after the journey by barge to another city, the statue would be carried up to the temple in procession, to pay the god of the host city an official visit.

Because Nippur was the city of En-lil, head of the Mesopotamian pantheon, delegations from other cities were often paying such visits, and Abram had sometimes been able to watch them arriving at the quayside and then advancing up to the temple in solemn procession.

Figure 5. A procession of Mesopotamian deities being carried from a temple. Bas-relief from the palace of Tiglath-pileser III, King of Assyria (ca. 740 BC). British Museum.

As Abram rounded the next bend in the river, the view to the northwest was no longer blocked by trees, so the city of Nippur could be seen for the first time.

Looking across the irrigated fields, the land was completely flat with a scattering of palm trees. But rising above this open vista, the city shimmered in the heat-haze like a mirage, seeming to float above the plain as if it was a low cloud. And poking through the centre of this cloud like a small mountain peak was the great ziggurat of Nippur, with the temple of En-lil a glittering jewel at its apex.

Figure 6. Reconstruction of how the ziggurat of Nippur may have appeared in the time of Abraham, based on ruins at Ur.

As Abram approached the city it became visibly rooted, rather than a floating mirage, but at the same time it appeared to rise up even higher above the plain. Soon he was below the city, looking up at imposing walls of brick surmounting a steep forty-foot-high bank of brown clay.

This earthen bank was the foundation on which the city was built, a thick pile of debris that was the result of nearly three thousand years of human habitation, combined with the constant disintegration of the un-fired clay bricks from which nearly all its buildings were constructed.

Nippur had grown up on either side of the ancient river, and its channel now cut right through the middle of the city between high earthen banks. But where it passed below the temple quarter there was a grand staircase that gave direct access to the sacred precinct, so that when the statues of the gods arrived by barge, they could be carried directly up the steps and into the temple.

The path from Drehem followed the river as it approached the city, and here Abram could see tall towers of kiln-fired bricks that stood on either side of the waterway like silent sentinels. Meanwhile, on the far side of the river, the tops of palm trees could be seen peeping over the city walls, marking the beautiful public gardens that filled the southern corner of the city.

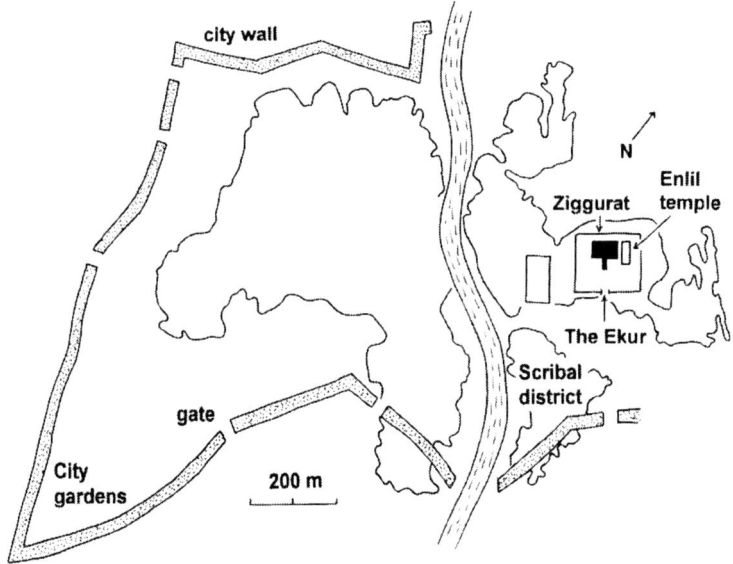

Figure 7. Map showing features of the city of Nippur as they may have appeared in the time of Abraham, based on modern excavations and an ancient map found in the scribal district of Nippur. Contour lines indicate heights 40 feet above the plain.

Finally, just before it reached the city walls, the path veered to the right and started to climb up towards the temple gate. Abram followed its upward curve, driving the small flock of sheep though the gate-way and into the temple quarter of the ancient city.

The road pressed straight onwards, up a gentle incline to an imposing gateway marking the entrance to the temple precinct itself. But behind the walls of the precinct, the grand stairway of the ziggurat could be seen marching upwards between lofty towers in three great flights. And at its top the stairway led to the upper platform of the ziggurat, on which stood the very House of God.

Figure 8. View of the great stairway of a Mesopotamian ziggurat, as it may have appeared at Nippur in the time of Abraham. Based on the partially restored Great Ziggurat of Ur.

As always, the House of God was gleaming in the intense light of a cloudless sky, with white plastered walls that dazzled in brightness. But guarding access to the temple precinct and the grand stairway were pairs of well-armed soldiers, blocking all admission. Only the priests were allowed to climb the stairway to the House of God, and then only bearing offerings of food and drink for En-lil. The penalty for unlawful trespass in the temple precinct was death.

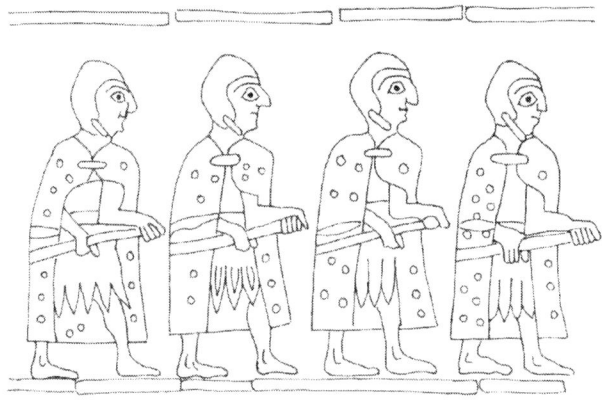

Figure 9. Soldiers in military dress around 2400 BC. Detail from the 'Standard of Ur', British Museum.

Other soldiers were guarding a new complex of buildings that lay immediately below the ziggurat. This complex had been commissioned by King Shulgi only a few years ago, and contained the Temple Library, the School of Writing, and the homes of the scribes.

The soldiers were in their ceremonial uniform, with either a decorated cape or a sash thrown over their pleated and frocked tunics. But they were grim-faced and armed with bronze swords and spears. Abram knew enough of the reputation of the temple guards to give them a wide berth as he drove the animals through a gateway on the opposite side of the street, which led to the animal pens for the temple sacrifices.

When the animals arrived, one of the temple attendants checked them to make sure that they had no defects, since it was a crime to present any animal in the temple that was not perfect. Then the attendant gave Abram a clay token to acknowledge the transaction, and his work for the day was over.

Abram had an hour or two of leisure before it was time for the journey home. Sometimes he went down to the city quayside to watch cargo barges from faraway places being unloaded. Sometimes he wandered into the market looking at the goods for sale. But his favourite pastime was to listen to the stories of the temple priests. Some of the stories, it was said, had been passed down by word of mouth since the creation of the world.

One old priest had no children to take care of him, and Abram had made friends with him by bringing gifts when the priest had been ill. He was so old that he could barely see, but he loved to spend a hot afternoon under a shady palm-tree in the city garden.

So Abram and the old priest had established a routine on the weekly visits when he delivered sheep to the temple. The old priest would take Abram's arm, and Abram would walk him across town to the gardens. This involved leaving the temple quarter, crossing over the river on a small ferry-boat, and walking through the back-streets of the city. But at the end of the last street, a wide gateway led into a green oasis of peace and tranquillity.

Here there were palm trees of all sizes and types, small fruit trees, flowering shrubs, and borders full of herbs, all divided into a neat patchwork with brick-paved walkways in between. There were also ponds between some of the walkways with fish in them. The ponds were held in basins of fired brick, cemented together with waterproof bitumen.

A small army of labourers was occupied in carrying water up from the river to fill the ponds and water the plants, since it almost never rained in Nippur. There was even a system of clay channels and small waterfalls, fed by a large cistern at the highest point in the garden. From the tiny waterfalls came the gentle sound of trickling water, a sound of incredible beauty and peace in the dry and parched landscape of the plains.

And beside each trickling water-fall, in shady spots beside the paths, there were seats for meditation or quiet conversation. Here, Abram and the old priest would settle down under an old palm-tree and the priest would tell stories of long ago that had been passed down through the generations.

Figure 10. Ancient Mesopotamian garden, such as was probably established at Nippur. Bas-relief from the palace of Ashur-banipal at Nineveh. British Museum.

Chapter 2

The Land Beyond the River

4000 years later, another story has been passed down through the generations. This is the story of how, in response to the command of God, Abram and his family set out from Ur of the Chaldeans to go to the Promised Land. At that time, Ur was the royal capital of an empire that covered the whole of the Mesopotamian plain and beyond, but today, much of the plain is a dried-up wasteland.

When the American forces crossed from Kuwait into Iraq in 2003 they were entering this land where Abram grew up, since the ruins of Ur lie only 100 miles northwest of the border, near the modern city of Nasiriyah. Another 100 miles to the northwest lie the ruins of ancient Nippur, and in a further 100 miles, the modern city of Baghdad.

These plains are the largest flat expanse on Earth, almost as flat as the sea. Today, the plains are largely a desert wasteland, covered only with waves of sand. But in the old days, when the spring floods caused the Euphrates to burst its banks, they became a true inland sea. And rising above this sea, like small man-made mountains, were the mounds that represent the only visible remains of ancient Mesopotamia.

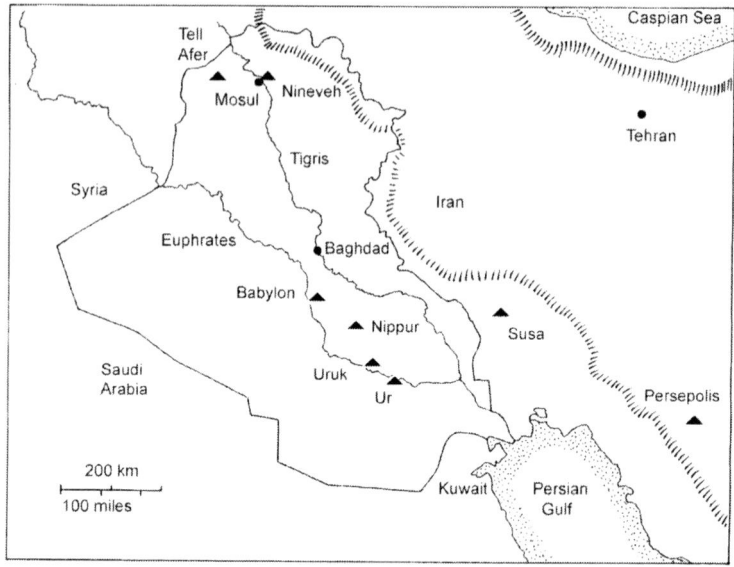

Figure 11. Map showing the modern political boundaries of Iraq and its neighbours. The plain of Mesopotamia lies between the Tigris and Euphrates (shown in their present day courses), and is flanked to the east by the Persian highlands.

This landscape was eloquently described by Austen Henry Layard, the nineteenth century archaeologist who is often called the Father of Assyriology. In his memoirs, Layard describes how he ascended the citadel mound of Tel Afer, located on the edge of the Mesopotamian plain in northern Iraq. In the evening sunshine, he looked out over this vast plain, stretching westward towards the Euphrates and losing itself in the hazy distance:

> *As the sun went down, I counted above one hundred mounds, throwing their dark and lengthening shadows across the plain. These were the remains of Assyrian civilization and prosperity. Now not even the tent of the Bedouin could be seen. The whole was a barren, deserted waste...*

Despite its desolate appearance, the Bible identifies this land as the birthplace of civilization. But when the Turks captured Constantinople in 1453, Europeans turned their backs on the Middle East for over 300 years.

However, there were always a few intrepid travellers who braved the dangers of the east to explore its mysteries. Typical of these was the Italian nobleman Pietro Della Valle, born in Rome in 1586. Unrequited in love, Della Valle turned to a friend from Naples for spiritual consolation and was advised that redemption from his dissolute lifestyle could be achieved by a making a pilgrimage to Jerusalem.

Della Valle set out from Venice in 1614, and after spending time in Constantinople and Alexandria, reached Jerusalem two years later. By then he had developed a taste for Middle Eastern adventure, and instead of returning to Italy he travelled eastwards to join the court of the Shah of Iran.

In 1617, Della Valle travelled through Mesopotamia and was one of the first Europeans to visit the ancient sites mentioned in the Bible. He was the first to correctly identify the ruins of Babylon sixty miles south of Baghdad, and he also visited Tell al-Muqayyar, the 'mound of pitch', later identified as the ancient city of Ur. From these ruins, Della Valle brought back to Europe the first samples of inscribed clay brick.

Later, while en route to the court of the Shah, Della Valle visited the ruins of Persepolis, the ancient Persian capital destroyed by Alexander the Great. Here he copied inscriptions written in the script we now call cuneiform, which he correctly identified as a form of ancient writing.

Pietro Della Valle finally arrived back in Italy in 1626 after twelve years of travels, during which time he had sent back more than fifty long letters to his friend in Naples. After his death these letters were published, providing one of the first written records of the archaeology of Mesopotamia and Persia.

Figure 12. The processional staircase at the Royal Palace of Persepolis, burned by Alexander the Great in 333 BC.

Unlike the monumental architecture of Egypt, the archaeological remains of Mesopotamia are relatively indistinct and unimpressive. Instead, it is the written record of ancient Mesopotamia that is most essential in reconstructing its history. Therefore, decipherment of the cuneiform script was crucial to progress in Mesopotamian archaeology. However, the key to its decipherment lay not in Mesopotamian itself, but in Persia.

Nearly two hundred years after Della Valle first copied the script at Persepolis, progress in its decipherment was made largely by three Danish scholars, Carsten Niebuhr, Friedrich Munter and Georg Friedrich Grotefend.

The first step was the recognition that there are actually three different types of cuneiform script at Persepolis. The second step involved identifying the simplest of the three scripts as a form of ancient Persian. Finally, a rough decipherment of the Persian script was achieved by recognising the names of the 5th century BC Archae-menid kings, Darius and Xerxes, in formulaic dedications such as the one shown below.

Figure 13. Part of one of the Old Persian texts from Persepolis, along with a Romanized transliteration in Persian and an English translation. Dots between signs are not in the original.

The text in Figure 13 was translated by Grotefend in 1802, but proof of the accuracy of his decipherment did not come until 1823, when Antoine Saint-Martin translated the Persian inscription on the Egyptian 'vase of Xerxes' (Figure 14).

Figure 14. Carved alabaster vase with three cuneiform scripts (the uppermost being Old Persian) along with the hieroglyphic rendering of 'Xerxes, great king'. Musée du Louvre.

Jean-Francois Champollion, the decipherer of Egyptian hieroglyphics, had already translated the cartouch on the vase as 'Xerxes, great king'. Saint-Martin was able to show, by comparison with the Persepolis inscription, that the Persian script on the vase was consistent with Champollion's reading of the cartouch. Hence, at least a limited decipherment of both hieroglyphics and cuneiform was demonstrated.

A definitive understanding of the Old Persian script was not achieved until the much longer inscription on the great rock of Behistun was copied and translated by Henry Rawlinson in 1846.

This inscription (Figure 15) was written in the same three scripts already seen at Persepolis, but being much longer, allowed a better understanding to be gained of its three languages.

At the same time, comparison with the material then being excavated from Mesopotamia allowed the identification of the peoples associated with each script. The second script was found to originate from the area around Susa, the homeland of the Elamites, whereas the third script was found to originate from northern Mesopotamia, the homeland of the Assyrians.

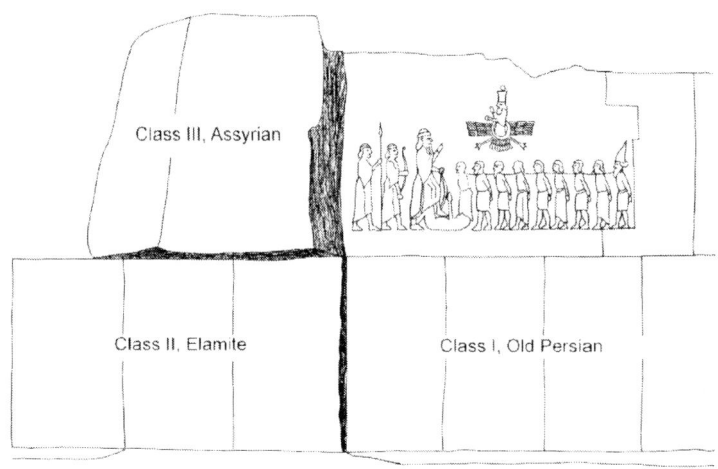

Figure 15. Simplified view of the inscription of Darius at Behistun showing the location of the three cuneiform scripts.

The decipherment of Assyrian was a slow and laborious process that depended on the contributions of many scholars. However, three particular individuals, Henry Rawlinson, Edward Hincks, and Jules Oppert made such major contributions that they have often been called the 'holy triad' of cuneiform studies.

By seeing how the names of kings and places were translated from Persian to Assyrian, these scholars were able to deduce the pronunciation of Assyrian, and concluded that it was one of the Semitic group of languages. However, the script was so appallingly complex, and had so many ambiguities, that other scholars doubted it was possible to properly understand it.

Eventually, in 1850, Hincks proposed an explanation for the clumsy complexity of the Assyrian script. It had not been invented by the Assyrians at all, but had been taken over by them from another race with a completely different language. The script had been invented for writing this other language, and was a 'forced fit' to express the Assyrian (Semitic) tongue.

Inscriptions in the other unknown language soon began to appear in new excavations from southern Mesopotamia. One of the first to be published (Figure 16) is important because it mentions the two principal regions of Mesopotamia, known in the Assyrian (Akkadian) language as Sumer and Akkad. Hence the unknown language was recognized as Sumerian.

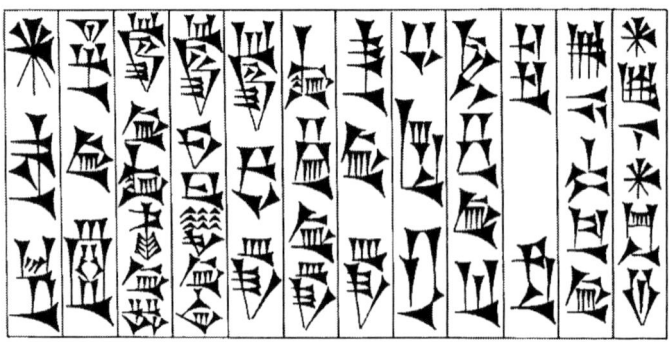

Figure 16. Text in Sumerian cuneiform inscribed on a brick from the temple at Isin and first published by Rawlinson. British Museum.

Considering that it was the Sumerians who invented writing, it is ironic that we still refer to them by the name 'Sumerian' that was given them by the Semitic peoples of northern Mesopotamia who stole their script.

Today, all that remains of ancient Sumer is a deserted wasteland, even more desolate than the remains of Assyria in the north. And it is this stark contrast, between the glories of ancient civilization and the bleak devastation of today, that has always affected western travellers most deeply. For example, when William Loftus first arrived at ancient Uruk (biblical Erech) in 1850, he was staggered by the sense of decay and abandonment that he experienced:

Of all desolate sights I even beheld, Uruk far surpasses all...

This very landscape was once the Garden of Eden, or, to be more exact, the garden *in Edin*, which is the Semitic name for the plains of Mesopotamia. And the Bible says that this garden was situated where four rivers met, two of which were the same Tigris and Euphrates that presently meet at Qurna, just 100 miles downstream from Uruk.

How did the Garden of God, Paradise on Earth, become a place of complete desolation? This is the story told in the Bible from Genesis to Revelation. But first we must see how it all began...

Chapter 3

The Story of Adam

Abram and the old priest were sitting in the city gardens of Nippur on a hot summer's day.

"What story shall I tell you?" asked the old priest.

"Tell me the story of creation, and of how God revealed himself to the first man."

So the old priest began, and Abram made the expected responses...

"On a faraway day..."   "Indeed, on a faraway day..."
"On a faraway night..."   "Indeed, on a faraway night..."
"In a faraway time..."   "Indeed, in a faraway time..."

"Before anything else existed, the Holy Gods existed: Anu, God of Heaven; En-lil, God of the Spirit; and En-ki, God of Wisdom; a Holy Trinity. So when Anu, En-lil and En-ki created the Cosmos, they made it in three parts. In a blinding flash, they separated the light of heaven from the darkness of the underworld, but in between them lay the formless empty earth.

"At that time there was no dry land; the earth consisted entirely of water. So the God of Heaven made a great dome to separate the water into two parts, with the sky in between. Then there were two seas; one on the earth below, deep and chaotic;

and one in the heavens surrounding the throne of God, like glass, as clear as crystal. And Anu was enthroned in the heavens above the sea of glass, but En-lil was hovering over the chaotic waters below, like a gentle wind.

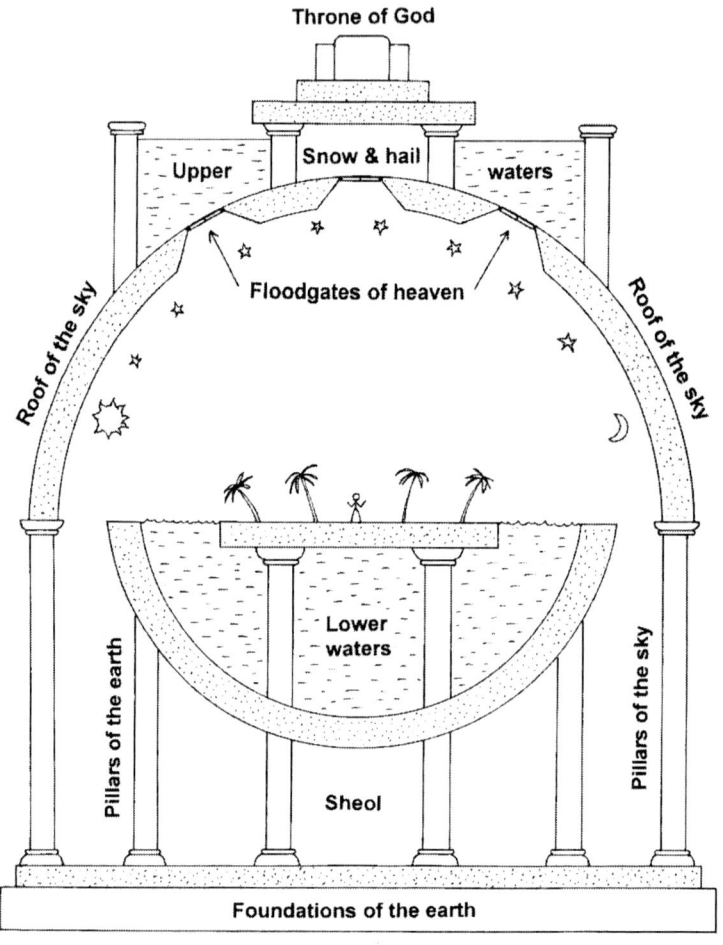

Figure 17. A visualization of the Cosmos as it appears to be described in the Bible.

"Then the Spirit of God brought order to the waters below by gathering them into one place so that dry land would appear, and the dry land brought forth plants. And then the Holy Trinity populated the Cosmos with the sun, moon and stars above; and with fish, birds and animals below. But there was still one thing missing; so the Holy Trinity made mankind in their own image; and then the Cosmos was complete."

The old priest had finished the story, but Abram did not want it to end so soon. "Yes, but what about the story of creation that you heard from the priests of Eridu, about how the God of Wisdom made the beautiful garden?"

So the old priest continued, "When Enki, God of Wisdom, made man, he was made from a mixture of the clay of the ground and the Spirit of God. And he was given a desire in his heart to know God."

But Abram interrupted, "How did man discover the Spirit of God and begin to worship him?"

The old priest answered patiently, "The God of Wisdom made man a living being, but man could not see God, so he searched for the Spirit of God in the mysterious powers of nature that generate all life...

Figure 18. Prehistoric cave paintings widely interpreted as an expression of the mysterious powers of nature. From the roof of the Hall of Bulls, Lascaux Cave, France, ca. 15,000 BC.

... the source of new life when a baby is born, when the lamb is born in the field, and when the seed sprouts in the springtime... Mankind knew that the Spirit of God was behind these mysteries, but he could not find God. So there were many long generations of fruitless search.

"However, God had a plan to reveal himself to mankind at the right time. And finally, when that time had come, God chose one special place on the earth where he would meet with a man for the first time. Then the God of Wisdom would take on human form, and would come to talk with the man and reveal the truth. And we call the man God chose 'Adam', which means simply... 'the man.'

"Where would God choose to meet with Adam and tell him the story of Creation?" asked the old priest, while Abram, in a reverie, was imagining the appearance of Wisdom. Abram sat up with a start, then looked around him at the beautiful well-watered garden, the trees bearing fruit, the flowering shrubs and herbs, and the refreshing pools of water. "In a garden like this!" he responded.

Figure 19. The Tree of Life is attended by Cherubim-like beings in a paradisical garden. Wall relief from the palace of Nimrud. British Museum.

"Yes!" agreed the old priest. "Enki made a beautiful garden where he would meet with the man. And because there was no rain in the garden, it was watered by a river. This river flowed across the plain, which is called 'Eden' and was fed by the great rivers, Tigris, and Euphrates."

Figure 20. A worshipper being introduced to Enki, God of Living Waters, whose overflowing vessels feed the rivers of Mesopotamia. Impression from a cylinder seal (ca. 2300 BC). Musée du Louvre, height 1 inch.

Abram stood up to consider what the old priest had said. From the highest part of the garden where they were sitting, you could look out over the city wall and see the Euphrates, the Great River itself, as it emerged from between the high walls of the city. And then, looking to the southeast, he could trace the river into the distance, as its border of palm trees stood out against the totally flat landscape. Far into the distance, beyond his home at Drehem, the mighty Euphrates flowed towards the eastern sea.[3] But where was the Garden of God?

Reading Abram's mind as he looked out across the plain, the

---

[3] The Persian Gulf; literally, 'the sea of the rising sun'

old priest remarked, "The Garden of God is lost in the mists of time, but some people believe that the Great River flows across the bottom of the eastern sea and then re-appears on an enchanted island called Dilmun."

Abram had heard of Dilmun, because traders came from that land in ships, and even brought precious shells and other gifts of the sea to sell in the cities of the South. However, he had no idea where Dilmun was.

The old priest continued, "It is said that if you are rich, you can pay to have your body taken to Dilmun[1] after you die, to be buried there. And people believe that if they are buried in Dilmun, they will rise from the dead to live with God in his garden, which is called Paradise - the Garden of God. However, I believe that the Garden of God was washed away by the sea, and will never be found again."

"What was it like when the God of Wisdom first revealed himself to Adam?" Abram wondered.

"That is a mystery," admitted the Priest, "One legend says that the dwelling place of God is at the furthest horizon of the sea, and another legend says that Wisdom came out of the sea in a great fish. But I believe that Wisdom came to man walking across the sea. He came six times to visit Adam, after six evenings and mornings, and he explained the mystery of how the Heavens and the Earth were created.

"But on the seventh day Wisdom did not teach Adam. On that day Adam worshipped God and rested in God's presence. And after that, the Spirit of Wisdom would come to talk to Adam in the cool of the evening every day. And in the presence of God, Adam experienced a wonderful rejuvenation, which is the fruit of the Tree of Life, so that he never seemed to age at all."

---

[1] By the time of Abraham, Dilmun was recognised as the island of Bahrein in the Persian Gulf.

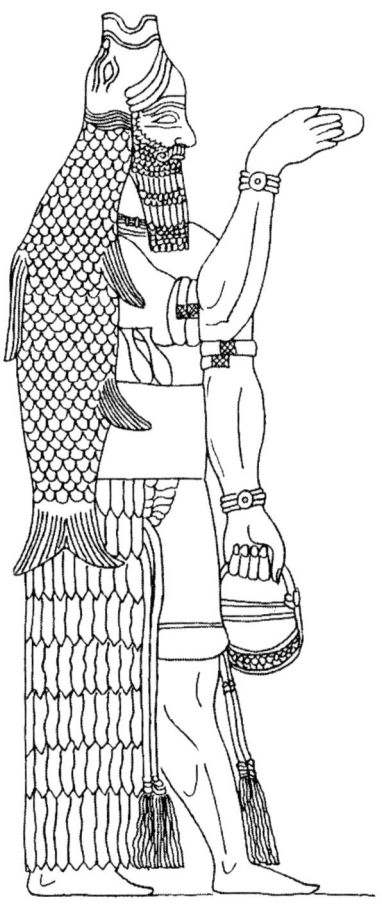

Figure 21. The legendary Mesopotamian 'Fish man'. Bas-relief from the temple of Nunurta at Nimrud, based on an engraving by Layard (1849).

"If only that was the end of the story..." the old priest reflected, "But there was another spirit in the garden who was God's enemy. This spirit was the fallen angel Lucifer, who had rebelled against God."

"Lucifer appeared to Adam and Eve in the form of a shining serpent. He said to Eve, 'You are just like one of the wild animals. You are completely dependent on God for the fruit of supernatural rejuvenation. But I can show you how to obtain supernatural knowledge that will make you self-sufficient, and not dependent on God.'

"When Eve considered this idea, it seemed very attractive. She forgot that God had warned her, 'Do not taste the fruit of independent knowledge, for the moment you cut yourself off from my Spirit, you will die.' So the woman tasted the thrill of independence from God, and she persuaded Adam to taste it as well. But as soon as they tasted the fruit, they both realised that their humanity was exposed and naked. They had cut themselves off from God's Spirit, and they realised that they would now shrivel and die."

Figure 22. Adam and Eve expelled from the Garden of Eden. Detail based on 'The Expulsion' by Masaccio, 1425 AD. Fresco from the Church of Santa Maria del Carmine, Florence.

"Then Wisdom appeared to Adam and Eve, and said, 'Because you broke your life-giving dependence on me, and followed the rebellion of Lucifer, you will no longer have free access to my presence. In future, you can only meet with me by first shedding the blood of a sacrifice, as a symbol of the death that your rebellion has brought.'

"So Adam took a sheep of the flock, and killed it as a sacrifice to God, and burned the flesh on an altar, as a symbol of the punishment that was due for breaking God's commandment. And when Adam did that, the Spirit of God appeared to him in the smoke of the sacrifice, as a symbol that his offering had been received. And then Adam worshipped the Lord, and the pain of his separation from God was lessened."

Figure 23. The Spirit of God receiving a burnt offering. Detail based on the 'Sacrifice of Abel' by Charles Mellin, ca. 1640. Oil on canvas, 12 x 15 inches, Musée Lorrain, Nancy.

Abram let out a sigh of relief. The pain and anguish in this story was so great that it cut him to the heart every time he heard it. He said this to the old priest, who replied, "That is because the Spirit of God is with you Abram. The Spirit of God has revealed to me that you are destined for a special purpose. You cannot become a priest as I am and enter the Holy Place of En-lil in the 'house of the mountain' but maybe En-lil will reveal himself to you in a dream and show you his purposes. In the meantime, you must return to Drehem, and to your father's house."

Chapter 4

The Rediscovery of Nippur

Nippur had a long history after the time of Abraham, and remained a holy city for hundreds of years. Gradually it waned in importance and became a backwater of history as empires came and went.... Assyria, Persia, Greece, Rome, and finally Islam.

Through all this time the land of Mesopotamia was still inhabited and the old ways of life continued, until the Middle East was invaded by the Mongol hordes in the thirteenth century AD. The Mongols devastated the cities and destroyed the complex network of canals that were the life-blood of Mesopotamia. The cities were left in ruins and the plain reverted to a desert wasteland.

When Austin Henry Layard visited the ruins of Nippur in 1851, they were known by their modern name of Nuffar and lay on the boundary between the hostile desert to the north and the vast marshlands of central Mesopotamia to the south. Layard excavated there for two weeks, but with little success.

Unlike the great palaces of Assyria, with their monumental stone sculptures and walls faced with bas-relief carvings, the earlier buildings of southern Mesopotamia were built almost entirely of mud bricks, many of them not even kiln-fired.

Excavating these mud-brick buildings was like digging for dirt amongst dirt, and there were few finds that would have excited the museum-going British public.

The only significant artefacts that Layard discovered at Nuffar were strange clay coffins, which tended to fall apart as soon as they were excavated. Eventually Layard recovered some complete examples (Figure 24), but it was later shown that these were from the Parthian era, around 200 AD.

Nuffar was a dangerous place to work, due to an almost perpetual state of war between the different tribes in the area. Layard's health deteriorated as a result of having to live in the marshlands as a guest of the local sheik. Finally his worsening health forced him to leave and he was glad to return to the more pleasant lands of the north.

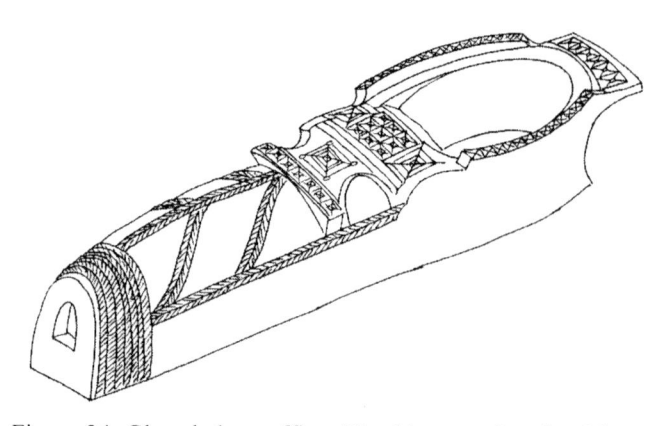

Figure 24. Glazed clay coffin of Parthian age found at Nippur and other southern Mesopotamian cities. British Museum.

Excavation work at Nuffar did not resume for nearly forty years, until the University of Pennsylvania undertook its first expedition to the mound in 1889. Nuffar was chosen as one of the largest un-excavated sites in southern Mesopotamia, and also based on its identification with the ancient city of 'Calneh', believed to be one of the centres of Nimrod's kingdom described in Genesis 10:10. In this identification the advocates of Nuffar were mistaken, but the city was indeed found to be one of the most important in the whole of Mesopotamia.

The expedition to Nuffar lasted, on and off, for more than ten years, and turned out to be a much larger undertaking than originally anticipated. Indeed, on first arriving at the mound, the impression was more of a 'picturesque mountain range' than the remains of an ancient city.

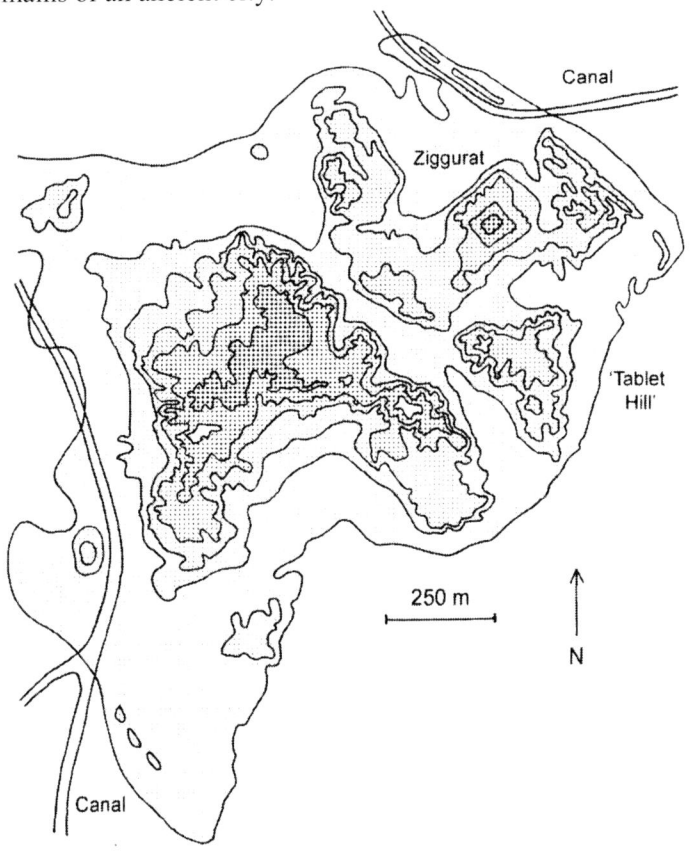

Figure 25. Map of the ruins of Nippur, contoured at 4m intervals, ranging from ca. 15m above sea level on the plain (white) to ca. 40m at the highest points (dark shading).

A survey of the mound showed it to be cut into two halves by the dried-up bed of an old canal (running NW-SE), now believed to have been the original course of the Euphrates River. In the eastern half, the highest point was marked by the site of the ruined ziggurat. Excavations were begun in this vicinity; however it was later realised that the ziggurat had been built over in the Parthian period to construct a fortress.

Many of the problems encountered by Layard were still present in 1889. The Afej swamps to the southeast of the city were still 'insect-breeding and pestiferous', while sandstorms from the desert to the northwest 'parched the human skin with the heat of a furnace'. In addition, there was dissention amongst the scholars of the expedition as to the best excavating technique.

The expedition leader, John Peters, was determined to carry out a comprehensive survey of the site, which involved digging large numbers of trenches, tunnels and shafts all over the mound. In contrast, the expedition philologist, Hermann Hilprecht, wanted to concentrate on a triangular mound to the south of the ruined ziggurat, which he thought the most likely site for the houses of the priests, the scribal school, and the temple library:

> *In close proximity to the sanctuary of Bel[2], open on all sides to the fresh breezes in the summer, and yet well protected from the rough north winds which swept down from the snow-capped mountains of Persia during the winter, this section of the ruins seemed to fulfil all the conditions required...*

Despite all of the problems, the first expedition recovered more than two thousand tablets over a six week period. However, Peters was less skilled than Layard at dealing with the local Arab population, which was particularly wild. As a result of this, the expedition was cut short when a looter was shot dead, causing

---

[2] Bel was the old translation of El-lil, which is En-lil in Sumerian

the Arabs to burn down the camp in retaliation. This led, on the next expedition, to the building of an incongruous-looking expedition house on the only defensible location: the top of the ruined ziggurat.

Figure 26. The ruins of Nippur at the present day, with the remains of the Pennsylvania expedition house standing atop the eroded ruins of the ziggurat, and 'Tablet Hill' in the foreground.

The second and third Pennsylvania expeditions continued to uncover large numbers of tablets from other parts of the site. However, the fourth expedition, in the year 1900, represented the crowning achievement of the work, when the scribal quarter ('Tablet Hill') was excavated in detail.

Hilprecht's vision of Tablet Hill, described above, seems more romantic than scientific, but his faith was vindicated, because the tablets recovered from this area were later shown to be particularly rich in literary material, and of much greater value than the many thousands of bureaucratic tablets recovered from other parts of the site. So much so, that the collection of around 2000 literary tablets from Nippur represents two-thirds of the known literature of the ancient Sumerians.

Another find of immense value was also made during the 1900 expedition. This was a clay jar dating from around the 6th century BC that contained a variety of much older objects. These had obviously been amassed by an ancient collector to make a miniature 'museum'. The collection consisted of twenty objects, including several inscriptions and a variety of tablets of different ages.

One of the most important items in the ancient collection was a precisely-drawn map of Nippur, inscribed on a clay tablet. The map is labelled with the name of the city as written in cuneiform: 'place of En-lil', and several features shown on the map are also labelled in cuneiform. These features on the map have been tied in with the results of modern excavation to provide a unique insight into the layout of the ancient city.

Another fascinating object from this collection, shown in Figure 27, was labelled on the back in Assyrian:

Mold of an inscribed stone, which Nabu-zerlischir the scribe saw in the palace of King Naram-Sin at Akkad

The translation of the Sumerian (modified after Hilprecht, with slashes separating panels of the inscription) is as follows:

Shar-gani-shah-ali / the powerful / king / of the subjects / of En-lil

Figure 27. Sumerian inscription from the collection of a scribe of ancient Nippur.

To better appreciate the early Sumerian script, the drawing of the mold in Figure 27 is shown as a mirror image. It therefore resembles the original inscription, reading from right to left. The middle panel (king) is a stylised view of a man wearing a crown, while the left hand panel is the Sumerian name of En-lil: the 'star sign' indicating divinity; an object that may be a throne, meaning 'Lord'; and a lattice-work meaning 'air' or gentle wind, i.e. 'the Breath of God'.

The number of literary tablets collected by the Pennsylvania expeditions to Nippur was so great that it took a whole century for the major part of them to be translated and understood. Drawings of some of the tablets were published by Arno Poebel in the early part of the 20th century, but the great difficulties in understanding the Sumerian language prevented meaningful translation.

These difficulties arise from the fact that Sumerian is not related to any known language, and is very different from the Semitic languages prevalent in the Middle East. Thus, even though the ancient scribes compiled Akkadian–Sumerian dictionaries, it took Poebel years to complete his great work, *Characteristics of Sumerian Grammar*.

The second great difficulty in reconstructing the ancient literature of Sumer was the very fragmented state of the tablets, which are mostly incomplete and broken into several pieces. Prior to publishing his landmark *Sumerian Mythology* in 1944, Samuel Noah Kramer devoted a decade of intense work to simply piecing together the tablets themselves.

One example of Kramer's diligence in reconstruction was the 'virtual' joining of two fragments of a literary tablet whose parts were located respectively in the University Museum in Pennsylvania, and the Museum of the Ancient Orient in Istanbul.

They had become separated because the permit to excavate Nippur stipulated that the artefacts recovered should be divided equally between the two museums. In view of the fragmentary state of the tablets, they were essentially shovelled into packing cases and then shipped at random to the two separate museums!

The long process of reconstruction of the mythological fragments is well illustrated by the history of another tablet, shown in Figure 28, which has been titled the Creation of Man. This tablet has been reconstructed from four fragments, of which parts 1 and 2 were joined and then published in 1919 by Stephen Langdon. Fragment 3 was later published in isolation by Edward Chiera. Finally, Kramer found the last fragment, joined them all together, and published a translation in 1944.

Published by Chiera (1934)

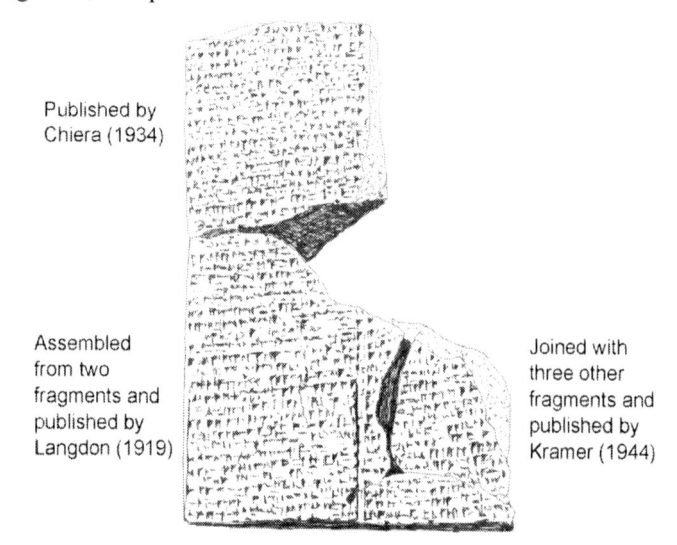

Assembled from two fragments and published by Langdon (1919)

Joined with three other fragments and published by Kramer (1944)

Figure 28. The front (obverse) side of the Sumerian myth 'The Creation of Man', to show its assembly from four fragments by Kramer. University Museum, Pennsylvania.

One of the most important literary works discovered at Nippur was the Sumerian account of the Great Flood (Figure 29). Drawings of this tablet were first published by Arno Poebel in 1914, but the text was not fully translated for several decades. It was finally included by Thorkild Jacobsen in his 1987 masterpiece of Sumerian poetry in translation, *The Harps that Once...*

Unfortunately, more than half of the Sumerian Flood Story is missing, and only one copy has ever been found, but this piece is sufficient to indicate a common source with the flood story in the Gilgamesh Epic, the most complete version of which was discovered by Layard's assistant, Hormuzd Rassam, in the great library of the Assyrian kings at Nineveh.

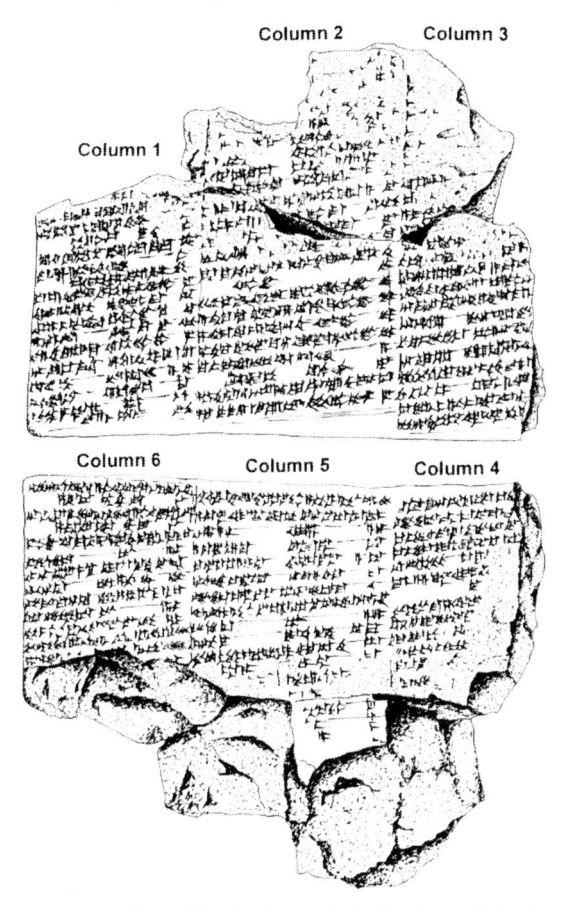

Figure 29. Drawing of both sides of the broken tablet bearing the Sumerian Flood Story. Based on drawings and photos by Arno Poebel. University Museum, Philadelphia.

The Gilgamesh Epic relates the heroic exploits of Gilgamesh, King of Uruk. After the death of Enkidu, his sparring partner and soul-mate, Gilgamesh sets out on a quest to find the lost secret of immortality, and is directed to search for the hero of the Flood, the Mesopotamian equivalent of Noah. His name, Ut-napishtim, means 'He found Life' because his obedience in building the Ark was rewarded with eternal life, *'in a faraway place at the mouth of the rivers'*. The fact that the place of immortality is located where rivers meet suggests that this is an echo of the Garden of Eden described in Genesis.

The account of the Great Flood in the Gilgamesh Epic was first translated by George Smith, a junior assistant at the British Museum who spent many years sorting and cataloguing Layard and Rassam's finds from Nineveh. In 1872, Smith presented his results in a lecture to the Biblical Archaeology Society that was attended by a distinguished gathering of London society, including the Prime Minister, William Gladstone.

At this lecture, Smith translated excerpts from the eleventh tablet of the Gilgamesh Epic, pointing out the remarkable resemblances with the account of Noah's Flood in the Bible. For example, both accounts describe the gathering of all living things aboard the Ark before the Flood, and the sending out of birds after the Flood to test the drying up of the flood-waters.

These similarities show beyond any doubt that the biblical and Mesopotamian versions of the Flood Story come from a common source. However, evidence from the literary tablets of Nippur shows that the Gilgamesh Epic (in Akkadian) was actually put together from half a dozen separate stories, originally written in Sumerian. Hence, we can conclude that the story of Noah's Flood was probably handed down in the Nippur priesthood for hundreds of years by word of mouth, until one day it was heard by Abraham...

Chapter 5

The Great Flood

It was the spring-time of Abram's twelfth year. The Euphrates had been rising for weeks as the snows melted in the mountains of the north. Finally, the river overtopped its banks and flooded the plain as far as the eye could see.

After a several days the water level started to go down again, but the low-lying land downstream from Drehem would remain flooded for months. This was an area where the Euphrates wound its way through mile upon mile of tall reeds, with many small channels that formed an impenetrable maze. And on small islands that rose above the marshes stood the reed-built huts of the cattle herders who tended the water-buffalo that roamed through the marshes.

Drehem was located on an area of slightly higher ground than the marsh, so during the spring floods it became an island in the middle of a shallow sea. But as the water went down, Abram had to drive his flock from Drehem to Nippur through knee-deep water and mud. Finally, he arrived exhausted, and after a wash, was glad to go round to the house of the old priest for a refreshing drink.

This year's flooding had been more extensive than for many years, and brought to mind the Great Flood of long ago.

Figure 30. A large reed-built house of the Marsh Arabs during flood time.

"Please tell me the story again," begged Abram.

"Very well," replied the old priest, even though he had told Abram the story a dozen times before.

"On a faraway day... after Adam was driven out of paradise, his sons learned to farm the fields and shepherd the flock, and they presented the fruits of the field and the firstborn of the flock as burnt offerings to God; and if the offering was acceptable, the Spirit of God would appear in the smoke of the sacrifice.

"It was in those days that men started to build the first cities, and so they built a house for God in each city, called the Temple of God. But it was not possible for all the people to offer sacrifices to God in the temple, so the descendants of Adam acted as priests, and they were responsible for taking the animals brought by the people and offering them as sacrifices to God on behalf of the people. So the priests lived in the temple and became separate from the rest of the people.

"After a while, the priests became proud of their special position. They said to themselves, 'If we live in the house of God, we must be the sons of God. We will find God a wife, and she will be the Mother Goddess, and we will be her children.' So the priests made a throne for the Mother Goddess in the temple, alongside the throne of God, and then they placed a bed in the temple for God to sleep with his wife."

Figure 31. Inanna, one of the female goddesses which exemplify the idolatry of the Sumerian priests. Clay relief, ca. 1750 BC; British Museum, height 18 inches.

"But then the Spirit of God was displeased, and did not appear in his temple any more, as he used to. So the priests said, 'We will take the place of God, and we will choose priestesses to take the place of the wife of God, and then we ourselves can produce sons for God.' And so the temple became a place of sexual immorality instead of the place where God's presence was revealed.

"Six hundred years passed[6], and the wickedness of Adam's descendants was so great that God was sorry that he had created Adam and revealed himself to him. Instead of the worship of the True God, the temples of the land were full of corruption. So God said, 'I will wipe Adam's descendants, whom I have created, off the face of the land.'

"However, there was one man of priestly birth who had not become corrupt. This man was called Noah; he worshipped Enki, the God of Wisdom, and taught all of his family to do the same. Therefore, Wisdom appeared to him in a dream to warn him about the impending disaster. Noah prayed to Enki, to show him what to do. Then Enki told him, 'There will be a great flood. You must tear down your house and use it to build a boat. Then you and your family will be saved when the flood comes.'"

"How could you build a boat from a house?" interrupted Abram, even though he had heard the story many times before.

"In those days," replied the old priest, "our ancestors did not live in houses built of clay bricks as we do today, but in houses built of reeds, like the cattle herders."

"How could reeds be strong enough to build a boat?" Abram wondered.

"Even today," replied the old priest, "you know that the cattle herders who live in the marshes build their houses entirely out of reeds. They bind them together into giant bundles, which

---

[6]The Sumerian equivalent of a thousand years...

they use to make thick pillars to hold up the walls and roofs of their houses. So Noah's family could have fastened the pillars of their houses together to make a huge raft of reeds, and then built another house on top. And they would have smeared tar on the reeds to make them waterproof, like the marsh people do."

"And how big was the ark that Noah built?" Abram asked, becoming interested now in the details of its construction.

"It had to be very large, 300 arm-lengths long and 50 arm-lengths wide, with a house three stories high, because apart from his own family, Enki told Noah to take seven pairs of each animal from his flocks and herds, and even a pair of each kind of animal from the wilderness."

Figure 32. Interior of a reed-built house of the Marsh Arabs, showing the giant bundles of reeds that form its structure.

"Then Anu, the God of Heaven, opened the flood-gates of the waters above the sky, and En-lil, God of the wind, sent a great storm, and it rained for longer than anyone could ever remember... forty days and forty nights. And the Great River burst its banks, and the underground springs gushed forth, and the water rose over all the land under heaven. The waters also rose above all of the temple mountains built by the priests, and all of their temples were washed away. And all the evil priests were drowned, and all the idols of the mother goddess were washed away. Every living thing on the surface of the land died, and only Noah and his family were saved, because they obeyed the command of Enki.

"But after five months the waters started to go down, and the ark finally rested on the foothills of the Aratta Mountains in the east. And when Noah looked out over the great plain, not one clay brick was left on top of another. All the temple mountains had been turned into mountains of mud and washed away, because in those days men had not invented kiln-fired bricks.

"But as soon as Noah had come out from the ark, he built an altar and sacrificed to God, to give thanks for his deliverance. And God received the offering, and promised that there would never again be a flood that swept away the whole land, even if men fell again into the same sins."

Moments of reverie passed while Abram's imagination was swept away to the far-off day when Noah had looked out of the ark for the first time, across the great empty plain that had once teemed with life. Then Abram suddenly blurted out, "Holy Father, when did the Great Flood happen?"

"Ah," said the priest, "it was as I said 'on a faraway day'. It was indeed in a far-off time, long ago."

"Yes, but how long ago really?" persisted Abram.

"That," said the old priest, "no-one knows, but according to the royal records, it was before the great dynasty of Kish."

That was indeed a long time ago, because Abram knew that before the great Empire of Ur in his own day, there had been the dark ages, when the Gutian savages had swept down from the mountains and destroyed everything on the plain. But before that there had been another great empire, the Empire of Sargon.

Sargon had conquered the whole world from the eastern to the western sea,[3] and before that there had been many long dynasties, going back at last to Gilgamesh, the great king of Uruk. And the dynasty of Kish was even before Gilgamesh.

Gilgamesh was an almost mythical figure. Had he even existed? If the Great Flood was before the dynasty of Kish, and that was before the time of Gilgamesh, it must indeed have been on a faraway day...

Figure 33. God accepts Noah's burnt offering after the Flood. Detail based on an engraving from *Die Bibel in Bildern* by Julius Schnorr von Carolsfeld, 1794-1872.

---

[3] From the Persian Gulf to the Mediterranean.

Chapter 6

The First Great Civilization

The succession of dynasties that stretched from the empire of Ur, all the way back to the time before the Flood, is listed in the great record of Sumerian civilization called the 'Sumerian King List'.

Under its first rulers, Ur-nammu and Shulgi, the empire of Ur witnessed a great renaissance of ancient Sumerian culture. Therefore, the King List was probably composed under their direction to link their new dynasty with the heroic age of ancient Sumer five hundred years earlier, which we call the Early Dynastic period.[8]

Gilgamesh finds his place in the Sumerian King List as a heroic king of the 'first dynasty of Uruk' in the middle of the Early Dynastic period. This was a time when the city of Uruk in the south of Mesopotamia was battling the city of Kish in the north for supremacy over the plain.

Although the many stories about Gilgamesh have raised him

---

[8] Historical tables are included in the appendix.

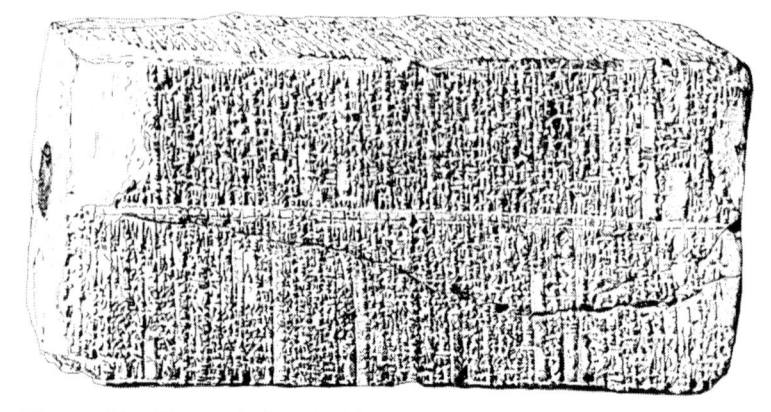

Figure 34. View of the Weld-Blundell prism, the most complete version of the Sumerian King List, in the orientation in which the script was originally read (vertical columns from right to left). Ashmolean Museum, Oxford; length 8 inches.

to almost mythical status, there are contemporary artefacts that identify some of the kings of Kish who reigned in this period. For example, a fragment of a stone bowl in the Iraq Museum names 'Me-bara-gesi King of Kish', a ruler who is attested by later literature to be a contemporary of Gilgamesh.

An even earlier inscription is found on a stone mace head now displayed in the Musée du Louvre. This mace head was presented as a temple offering, and reading from right to left, the primitive characters name the worshipper as 'King of Kish, Me-salim'. The pictogram for king is the same stylised picture of a man wearing a crown that was seen before, while the symbol for Kish is a long vertical wedge with a lozenge to the top right and a series of vertical strokes to the left.

According to the Sumerian King List, Me-salim was the last king in the great dynasty of Kish established 'after the Flood'. The King List also names five cities that ruled over the land of Sumer 'before the Flood': Eridu, Bad-tibira, Larak, Sippar and Shuruppak.

Figure 35. Large offertory mace head, decorated with lions and showing the worshipper as 'Me-salim, king of Kish' (ca. 2700 BC). Musée du Louvre; height 7.5 inches.

Curiously, the city of Uruk is not even mentioned in this list of antediluvian cities, although we know from archaeological evidence that between the founding of Sumerian civilization at Eridu and the establishment of the first dynasty of Kish, the city of Uruk was the centre of world civilization for nearly a thousand years. However, since the King List was compiled hundreds of years after the foundation of these cities, it is not surprising that earlier events were lost in the mists of time.

Archaeological remains at Uruk and Eridu actually form a continuous record that goes back more than 2000 years before the time of Gilgamesh. However, this record shows no sign of interruption by a cataclysmic flood, although there is evidence for some more local floods. Therefore, the Great Flood probably occurred *before* the foundation of Eridu, more than 5500 years BC, but became confused with a later flood that occurred shortly before the rise of Kish around 2800 BC.

In order to understand the earliest development of Sumerian civilization, we must look at the archaeological record at Eridu, which was systematically excavated by Seton Lloyd and Fuad Safar over a period of several years, beginning in 1948.

Lloyd and Safar recognised a total of 19 separate levels which could be dated by the characteristic pottery of different periods (see the appendix). Within those levels they discovered a remarkable sequence of superimposed temple structures, with progressively smaller temple buildings as they dug deeper.

This succession of temples can be distinguished because of the reverence shown by the Sumerians for the holy ground of the temple site. When they wanted to build a new temple they would only partially demolish the old walls, which were then filled with clay bricks, sand, or building debris to make a platform on which the new structure was built.

Successive temples were therefore built on successively higher platforms, which are shown in the accompanying diagram. Based on the ages of the pottery fragments found within the different levels, these temple structures were the result of more than 1500 years of development.

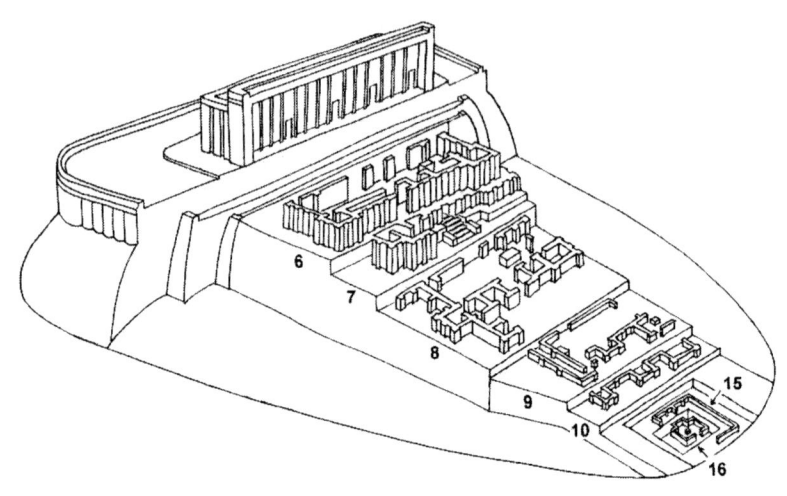

Figure 36. Exploded view of successive stages of temple building at Eridu. Modified after Heinrich and Seidl (1982).

The earliest clearly recognisable temple at Eridu (level 16) consisted of a single room only 10 feet square built of mud brick, with an altar in a niche on one side and an offering table in the middle. However, by the time of the level 7 structure around 1000 years later, the temple had a central 'nave' more than 50 feet long, containing a large altar at one end and an offering table at the other. In addition, there were many storage rooms down the sides of the building.

It is at this time, around 4300 BC, that the archaeological record begins in the city of Uruk, located 40 miles northwest of Eridu on the main channel of the Euphrates. This site was excavated systematically by German archaeologists over much of the twentieth century, and the work has been summarised by Hans Nissen.

A total of 18 different levels were recognised, showing that in a thousand year period from 4300 to 3300 BC the temples at Uruk grew progressively larger with time, following in the footsteps of Eridu. However, during this time, Uruk gradually eclipsed Eridu in importance, probably because its location on the Euphrates gave it better access to water for irrigation.

By 3300 BC, Uruk had reached the zenith of its cultural achievement. It was here that writing was first invented, and here also that major innovations were made in temple architecture.

One of these innovations was the cone-mosaic method of wall decoration. Coloured cones were made, about six inches long and two inches in diameter, either from stone or painted clay. These were pressed into a coating of wet clay that was plastered onto the mud brick temple walls, creating a variety of dazzling multi-coloured patterns.

This technique was particularly useful for the decoration of curved surfaces, and was used to face the earliest known examples of free-standing columns in the 'pillar hall' of the Eanna Complex.

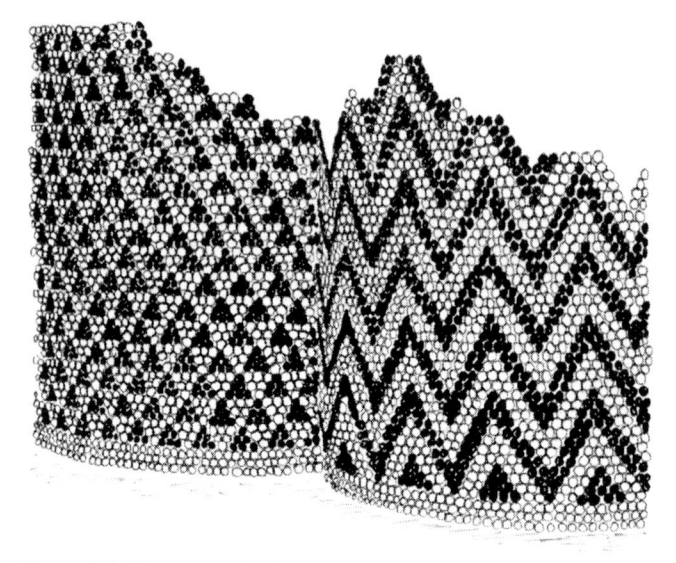

Figure 37. Cone mosaic decoration of the world's first columns.

The Eanna Complex was the cultic site of Ishtar,[9] Queen of Heaven, and consisted of a gigantic raised platform over 200 yards long bearing several immense buildings. These included a giant square storehouse built round a central courtyard and several great temples, the largest of which had a nave 150 feet long.

This was truly a 'cathedral city' in its scale of temple architecture, as well as an engine of immense economic power. This power was doubtless responsible for the elevation of Ishtar from a minor agricultural deity to become the 'wife' of Anu, God of Heaven. This eventually led to the eclipse of Anu himself, so that by the time the Gilgamesh stories were written, over 1000 years later, Ishtar rather than Anu was regarded as the patron deity of Uruk.

---

[9] Inanna in Sumerian.

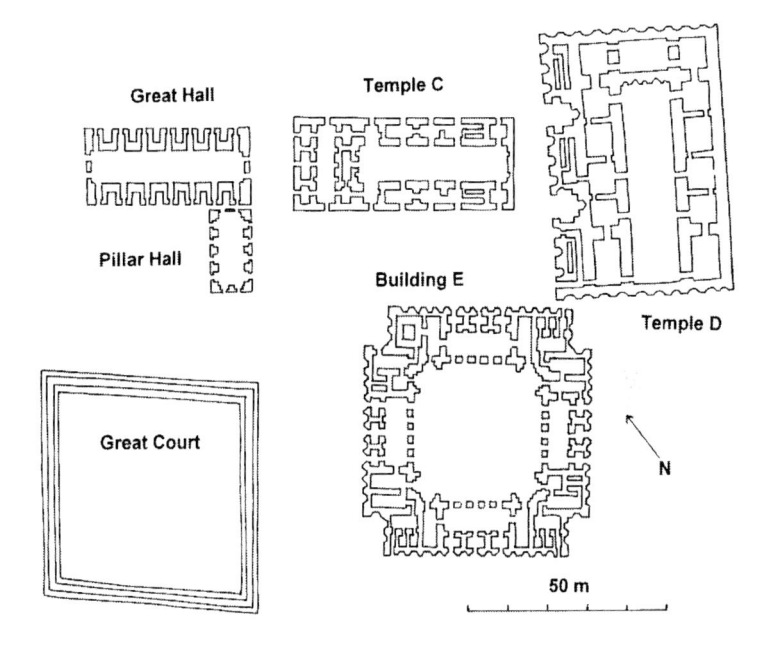

Figure 38. The Eanna complex of Uruk showing several great temples that were built within a few decades around 3200 BC.

Chapter 7

The Story of the Tower

Abram was sitting with the old priest in the temple precinct at Nippur, near the bottom of the great stairway that climbed the ziggurat. "Will you tell me the story of the tower that reached to the heavens?" he asked the priest.

"I've told you so many times before..."

"Yes," replied Abram, "but I want to hear how it was that God came to live in the Temple of the Mountain at Nippur."

So the old priest began... "In a faraway time... after the Great Flood had dried up from the land, Noah and his sons settled on the plain between the rivers.

"Noah made sacrifices to God, and he prayed to the God of Wisdom to show him where to build a city. So God showed him a place in the east, next to a beautiful lake full of sweet water. And Noah built a city and named it Eridu, which means the Good City. And God blessed Noah and his sons with wild game and fish and good harvests, so that their families multiplied greatly.

"Then they spread out from the east, moving up the branches of the Great River, and each family founded a different city on the bank of the river. Firstly there was Uruk (which we call Erech), and then Ur and Bad-tibira. And then moving further up the river, Shuruppak and Nippur and even Sippar in the northwest part of the plain.

"In those days there was universal peace and harmony. Everyone in the whole land between the rivers spoke one language, and there was no fighting between the cities, because they were all descended from one family. And in each city, they built a temple to worship God."

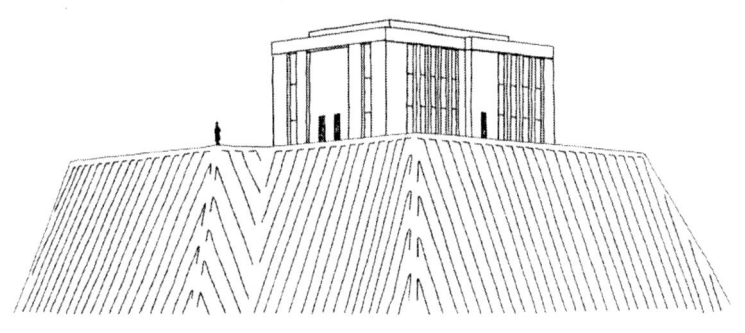

Figure 39. Reconstruction of the Anu ziggurat of Uruk, with its White Temple, probably plastered with gypsum to make it sparkle in the sun.

"But then rivalry began between the cities. Each city wanted to build a temple that was more glorious than the other cities. So they decided to knock down the old temples, and build ever larger ones on top of the old ruins."

Abram looked up at the great ziggurat of Nippur, and to the house of En-lil at its top. The temple gleamed in the evening sunlight, which was reflected off its white plastered walls like a great jewel. Could it be that the desire to build great temples to glorify the God of Heaven had led to rebellion against the very god they sought to exalt?

"At first, all was well," continued the old priest. "In the early days the priests of the great temples taught the truth to the people, of how Anu, En-lil and Enki were a Holy Trinity, united as one. But when rivalry began between the cities, each city started to worship a different member of the Trinity. In Uruk they worshipped Anu, the God of Heaven; in Nippur, En-lil, the Spirit of God; and in Eridu, Enki, the God of Wisdom and the Son of Anu.

"But then some of the priests of God repeated the great evil that had been done before the Flood. They said that if God was a father, and had a son, God must have a wife. So they chose a wife for the God of Heaven, and called her the Queen of Heaven. And as a sign of her divinity, they chose the emblem of the Evening Star."

Figure 40. Emblems of the astral deities (Venus, Moon-god and Sun-god) supersede the horned altars of the Sumerian Trinity on the top of a Babylonian stele. British Museum, height 18 inches.

"And likewise at the same time, the priests in other cities started to worship the sun and moon. So they created their own trinity of gods in the heavens to rival the trinity of the True God. And to exalt the name of Ishtar, Queen of Heaven, the priests decided to build her a temple in Uruk that would be higher than the temple of Anu. And so the priests built the temple of Ishtar on the opposite side of the river, on a high platform that they called Eanna (the House of Heaven).

"Now in those days the city of Uruk was the greatest city in the world, and the storehouses of Ishtar contained the greatest wealth in the world. And the peoples of the world would come to Uruk to trade their goods and to learn the secret of writing that the priests of Uruk had invented. So all the world learned the language of the priests of Uruk, which we call Sumerian."

Figure 41. The produce of the land is brought to the great storehouses of the temple of Inanna, as depicted on the upper register of the 3-foot high 'Uruk Vase.' Iraq Museum.

"Then the council of the gods (Anu, En-lil and Enki) discussed what the men were doing. And they said, 'If the priests of Uruk, to whom we gave the revelation of God, abandon the knowledge of the True God, and exalt the Queen of Heaven in the place of the True God, then they will be able to destroy the knowledge of God in all the Earth.'

"But God also remembered that he had promised, 'Never again will there be a flood that will destroy all life on the Earth, even though the heart of man is completely evil.' So instead of a flood, God raised up the Semitic people of the north, and established the kingdom of Kish in the north of the plain to be a rival for the city of Uruk in the south. Then the priests of Uruk stopped building the House of Heaven, because division came to the land between the rivers."

"But how did the temple of En-lil become the meeting-place for the Council of the Gods, and the most important in the whole land?" asked Abram.

"King Etana was the first king of Kish to conquer all of the northern plain. He subdued the other cities of the land, and built himself a royal palace at Kish to be the centre of his kingdom. But when he prayed to the gods for permission to build a temple, the omen said that the temple should be at Nippur, not Kish. So Etana began to build the first great ziggurat of En-lil at Nippur, although it was not finished for many years. And after it was built, people came from all over the plain to worship En-lil, the Spirit of God, in this temple.

"But after a long time the power of Kish began to wane, and the temple of En-lil fell into disrepair. Then Uruk regained supremacy over the cities of the plain under the rule of the great king, Gilgamesh. And when he sought an omen to build a temple for the gods, the omen said that he should rebuild En-lil's temple at Nippur. And so the temple was kept in good repair for hundreds of years.

"And even after Sargon conquered the whole land and established Akkad as the capital of a great empire, En-lil was still worshipped as Lord of the Four Quarters of the World, and his temple at Nippur was still revered. Until the time of Naram Sin... but what happened after that is something that I prefer not to talk about..."

Chapter 8

The Invention of Writing

As the temples of Sumer grew larger and larger, there was a growing need to keep track of the collection, storage and distribution of food. Thus began the world's first great bureaucratic system, whose earliest development at Uruk was revealed by the work of Denise Schmandt-Besserat.

In the days before writing was invented, records were kept using clay tokens. Each commodity had a different shaped token and each item was identified by one token unit. For example, a sheep was represented by a round token with a cross on it, and a jar of oil was represented by a miniature model of a jar. A transaction could be recorded by pressing the requisite number of tokens into a clay ball and then sealing the ball with a stamped impression.

The first major development of this record-keeping method at Uruk probably involved the innovation of drawing a picture of the tokens onto a clay tablet, rather than pressing the actual tokens into the tablet. This would have saved a lot of time by avoiding the laborious manufacture of tokens. However, the second development was even more important. The scribes realised that instead of drawing a picture for every token, they could draw only one picture and then mark a number of indentations next to this picture to signify the quantity. This single innovation heralded the separate development of counting and writing.

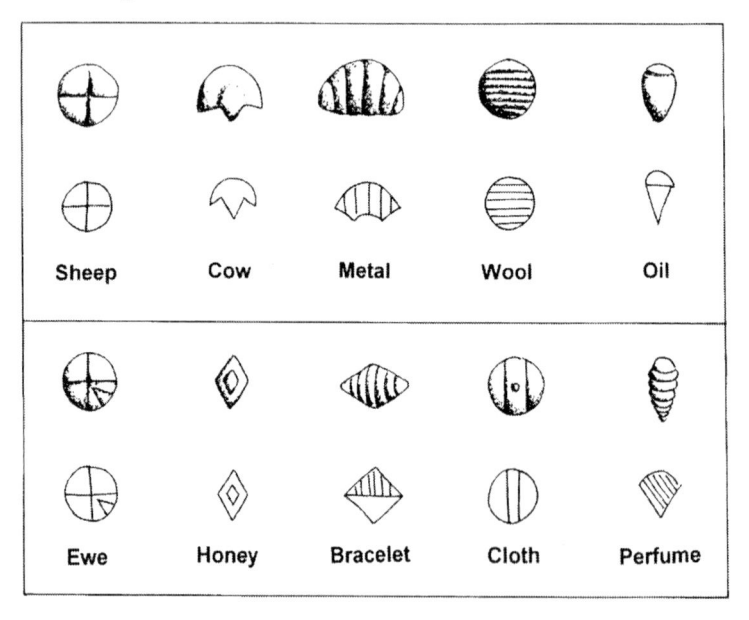

Sheep	Cow	Metal	Wool	Oil
Ewe	Honey	Bracelet	Cloth	Perfume

Figure 42. Evolution from tokens to protoliterate pictograms.

These changes began around 3500 BC (the Late Uruk period) and soon hundreds of 'pictograms' had been developed, each of which represented a whole word of the Sumerian language in picture form. These pictograms were developed and refined over the following two to three hundred years, appropriately called the Proto-literate period.

It is from this period that the first 'word lists' date, and these give us the first written evidence about Sumerian civilization; albeit in a highly codified manner. For example, the 'standard list of professions' lists dozens of occupations in a generally decreasing order of importance, beginning with a 'priest-king' who ruled the temple. These early word lists soon became a vital tool in scribal education, and hence were copied as exercises for hundreds of years. For today's scholars they provide a valuable window on the evolution of the Sumerian script over time.

As time went on, methods were developed to make the writing of pictograms faster. Instead of laboriously inscribing a line-drawing of an object, it was instead represented by pressing a stylus into the clay in a series of wedge-shaped marks... hence the development of the 'cuneiform' (wedge-shaped) script. In addition, to further speed up the writing process, the tablet itself was later turned on its side.

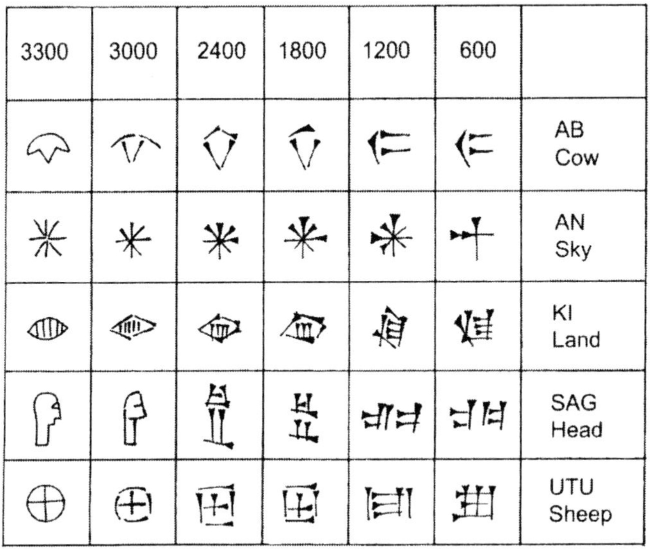

3300	3000	2400	1800	1200	600	
						AB Cow
						AN Sky
						KI Land
						SAG Head
						UTU Sheep

Figure 43. Evolution from protoliterate pictograms to cuneiform.

This completed the transformation of pictograms from clear drawings of objects into completely abstract patterns. However, the rotation of the tablet did not occur as early as once thought.

For example, the law code of Hammurabi (dating from ca. 1750 BC) is written with the cuneiform signs still in the original vertical columns.

A major problem with pictographic writing is the difficulty of representing abstract concepts, without which it is impossible to capture the 'spoken word' in writing. Pictographic writing can be used to convey simple instructions, such as 'take two sheep to the temple of Ishtar', but it cannot be used to write literature. Therefore, for writing to progress further, another step of development was needed. This was the invention of 'phonograms'.

Figure 44. Protoliterate age tablet recording the delivery of two sheep to the temple of Ishtar (totem pole sign on the left).

Sometime around the end of the Late Uruk period, when writing had become established as a reliable means of book-keeping, scribes probably encountered the need to record the names of people who were contributing temple offerings. Perhaps some of these people were foreigners from the north or east of Sumer whose names could not be expressed in Sumerian pictograms.

It must have occurred to some ingenious scribe that a name which could not be written directly could nevertheless be 'spelled out' phonetically. This was done by borrowing a group of otherwise unrelated words which had the same sound as the syllables of the name they were trying to pronounce. We can illustrate the process with the name of Hammurabi, King of Babylon, even though this comes from a later period. Hammurabi is a Semitic name but was written in Sumerian by writing each syllable of the name phonetically, as spelled out thus: 'Ha-am-mu-ra-bi'.

An example of the development of a phonogram to convey an abstract concept is provided by the Sumerian word for 'arrow' (*ti*) which apparently sounded the same as the word for 'life'. Hence, in an inscription from the Protoliterate period, we read '*En lil ti*'. Based on comparison with other similar inscriptions, the deduced meaning is: 'The Lord (*En*) breath (*lil*) is life (*ti*)'.

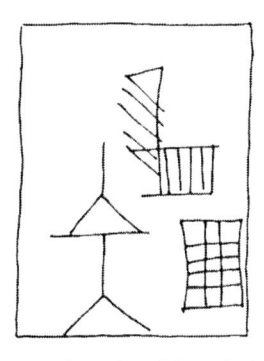

Figure 45. Protoliterate devotional inscription using a phonogram.

The words 'life' and 'arrow' are homophones in Sumerian, but not in Semitic languages such as Akkadian. Therefore, we can deduce from such examples that it was the Sumerians who made the step from pictographic to phonetic writing. Thus, by adapting a pictogram to make a phonogram for every syllabic sound in Sumerian speech, the Sumerians opened up to themselves the opportunity of expressing the total meaning of their spoken language in writing.

Although this development occurred near the beginning of the Protoliterate period, it took hundreds of years before writing progressed to the point where it could be used to write works of literature. This was partly because no-one saw the need to write literature. Most Sumerian myths and epics have a repetitive structure which suggests that they were transmitted orally rather than in writing. The repetitive nature of the story acts as a memory aid and is pleasing to the ear when orally recited.

When these oral traditions were finally written down, their repetitive structure was preserved. For example, in the very earliest collections of literature, discovered in the ancient city of Shuruppak and dating from around 2600 BC, several tablets begin with an introduction which was standard for later mythological texts:

> *On a faraway day, indeed on a faraway day,*
> *On a faraway night, indeed on a faraway night,*
> *In a faraway time, indeed in a faraway time...*
>
> [trans. Biggs, 1966]

One of the tablets bearing this text can be identified, from its style, as a school tablet copied as an exercise. The discovery of this form of introduction in a school tablet implies that it already had a long history before 2600 BC.

It seems staggering that texts written more than 4600 years ago should begin with an introduction that suggests a people who were themselves looking back into the mists of time. However, if the Flood did occur around 5500 BC, this was nearly 3000 years earlier than the school exercise text, ample time to conjure the phrase *'On a faraway day...*

Chapter 9

The History of the Temple

Even though the cuneiform name for Nippur means 'place of En-lil', there were many temples to other gods and goddesses in the city. For example, there was a temple dedicated to the 'wife' of En-lil, named Ninlil, and even a large temple dedicated to Ishtar, Queen of Heaven. In addition to these cultic sites, the temple precinct of En-lil itself contained two temple buildings, one on top of the ziggurat... the House of the Mountain... and one at the base of the ziggurat... the audience chamber of En-lil.

Abram had entered the temple at the base of the ziggurat with his father when they paid their yearly visit to lay votive offerings before the gods. The central space in the temple was shaped like the king's audience chamber, and on one side were three golden thrones on a raised dais. They were seated in front of a golden table, along the sides of which several smaller thrones were set. On the golden table in front of the thrones were many votive objects that worshippers had left as sacrificial offerings: small statuettes, offering bowls containing incense, and tablets bearing prayers.

The three great thrones were for Anu, En-lil and Enki. Two

golden statues, representing Anu and En-lil, sat on the middle and left-hand thrones, but the right-hand throne was empty. However, Abram's father had told him about the great day when the golden statue of Enki had been brought from his temple at Eridu to the grand council of the gods at Nippur. This usually only happened once in a lifetime, when the new king received his divine authority to rule from the council of the gods.

Figure 46. King Ur-Nammu pours a drink offering to the Moon-god. The audience chamber of En-lil at Nippur probably had similar statues of the gods on thrones. Detail from the Stele of Ur-Nammu. University Museum, Philadelphia.

Nobody except the priests could ascend the great staircase to the top of the ziggurat where the House of En-lil was situated. This was the very dwelling place of God, but in the completely-dark Holy of Holies, the throne of En-lil was empty.

However, as the old priest had described to Abram, "The throne of En-lil is intricately carved, and on the wall above and behind the throne there is a carved relief of a many-horned headdress, the mark of divine authority. And according to ancient tradition, a glowing cloud, the very Presence of God, used to occupy the throne, long ago."

"When was that?" wondered Abram.

"Those were the days," replied the old priest, "before the Gutian savages invaded the plain and destroyed all of the temples of Sumer."

Abram knew a bit about the 'Dark Ages' as they were called, the time when there was no law in Mesopotamia and every petty warlord did as he pleased. Then, after decades of anarchy, Ur-Nammu had restored order and brought the whole land under the rule of Ur. It was said that the Gutian invasion was the punishment of God on Naram-Sin, who had desecrated the temple of En-lil.

"I would like to hear again the story of Naram-Sin," pleaded Abram.

"That," replied the old priest, "is the worst story of treachery and disaster in our history, and I wish I had not mentioned it. But since it is a sobering lesson, I will tell you the story called 'The Curse of Akkad' so that you may learn its lesson...

"On a faraway day, the King of Kish had a cup-bearer named Sargon. Now the land had been conquered by a king from the city of Umma, called Lugal-zagesi. But this king did evil in the sight of God, desecrating the temples of the land. So God raised up Sargon to be a mighty conqueror, and in a few years he had defeated all the armies of Sumer. Then Sargon founded a new city that he called Akkad, and he made it the capital of a great empire.

"Sargon had a long reign, but eventually his sons, and then his grandson Naram-Sin, succeeded him as King of Akkad. Naram Sin was an even greater warrior than his grandfather, subjugating the whole earth from the eastern to the western seas. And the wealth of the empire that flowed to Akkad was so great that there was no room to store all the treasure that piled up."

Figure 47. Stele of Naram-Sin the warrior, whose horned helmet indicates divine status. The stele bears two inscriptions: a badly damaged original (top left) and a much later one (top right) written by Elamite raiders who carried the stele to Susa. Sandstone, 6 feet high, Musée du Louvre.

"Then Naram-Sin conceived a plan to build a great new temple at Akkad for Ishtar, the Queen of Heaven. And to glorify the new temple, he planned to use the treasures from the house of En-lil at Nippur. So, following the prescribed method, he sought an omen to demolish the temple of En-lil in order to use its treasures for the new temple, but the omen was negative.

"Seven times, Naram-Sin asked for an omen to demolish the house of En-lil, and seven times the omen was negative. So finally, having exhausted his patience, Naram-Sin did the unthinkable: he falsified the omen and sent his army to Nippur to destroy the temple of En-lil, as if he was sacking one of the cities of his enemies. He exposed the secret place, the Holy of Holies of En-lil, to the light of day, so that everyone could see its nakedness; he cut down the sacred temple trees, and he beat the sacred drinking vessels of God into scrap metal."

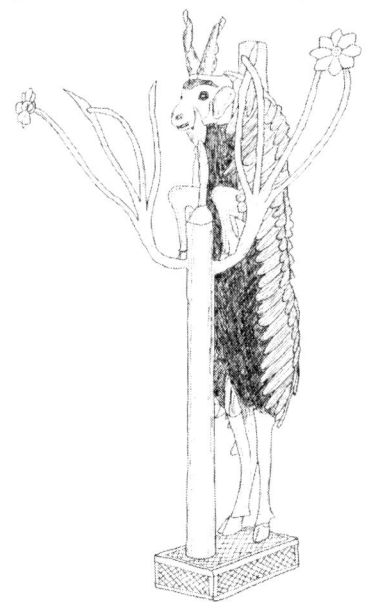

Figure 48. Sacred gold-covered tree from the royal tombs of Ur. Height two feet. British Museum.

"After this, an ominous silence fell on the whole plain of Sumer, as, full of foreboding, the whole land waited with bated breath to see if God would bring punishment. At first, it seemed as if life went on as usual, but gradually troubles increased more and more. The rains did not come in the northlands, so that the Great River did not rise in its spring flood. Then there was not enough water to supply the fields, and the harvests failed. And then the Gutian savages started to sweep down from the mountains and ravage the cities of the plain.

"Naram-Sin died, and his son reigned in his place, but gradually the Gutians overran more and more of the plain, until eventually they captured Akkad and burned it to the ground. And meanwhile the temple of En-lil at Nippur remained in ruins, and the whole land was desolate for more than a hundred years. Then finally, Ur-Nammu defeated the Gutians and began to rebuild the temples of the land, and his son, the great king Shulgi, restored the temple of En-lil that you see today."

Figure 49. Ur-Nammu (centre) takes the guise of a labourer, with pick-axe and carrying basket, to demonstrate his piety in rebuilding the temples of Sumer. Detail from the Stele of Ur-Nammu. University Museum, Philadelphia.

On his way back home from Nippur, Abram was thinking to himself, "I can never become a priest. Only the sons of priests can become priests. The Holy Father's family have been priests for generations, going back into the mists of time. But only the priests can go into the Holy Place at the top of the ziggurat and meet with En-lil, so how can I learn more about God?"

Abram was frustrated, but the old priest was philosophical. "Abram, you must be patient. The Lord En-lil has been worshipped in this temple at Nippur for more than 500 years. If you have a part to play in the plan of God, you will have to wait until the time is right. Then maybe God will reveal himself to you in a dream, and show you how you can serve him…"

Chapter 10

The Call

Those were the last words that the old priest said to Abram before he died. Years passed. The profound questions of youth faded into distant memories as Abram took over the day-to-day running of his father's livestock business. His father had become very rich in the service of the king, as one of the principal suppliers of sacrificial animals for the temples of Nippur and of other cities. Then came a summons to the royal court...

In response to the summons, Terah, Abram, and the whole family moved from Drehem to Ur, the imperial capital. Abram's father was now to advise the royal court on the procurement of livestock for the temples of the land. And he would go to the great ziggurat of Ur and join in the worship of the Moon-god, Nanna (Sin in the Semitic tongue).

But Abram could not forget all the stories that the old priest had told him in his youth. Of how the Lord En-lil was the true Spirit of God, and how the Moon-god was only a stone statue, without the real power of a god. But Abram did not speak of this to anyone.

Then, after nearly fifty years on the throne, the great king died. His sons and then his grandson succeeded him as king, but storm-clouds were gathering over the empire. The immigration of Semitic nomads from the northern steppes, which had been only a trickle when Abram's family had come to Sumer, had now grown into a flood. And the new immigrants were coming in armed bands to raid the prosperous cities of the plain.

At first the imperial armies were easily able to deal with the raiders, but as their numbers grew they started to overwhelm the defenders on the northern fringes of the empire. Trade was disrupted, and in the capital city, food became so scarce that the price of barley rose to more than ten times the price it had been a few years earlier.

As conditions in Ur started to deteriorate, Terah decided to migrate back to his homeland in the north. The city of Haran, on one of the upper tributaries of the Euphrates, was his chosen destination. It was closely linked to Ur by the trade route along the Great River, and by a similar devotion to the Moon-god.

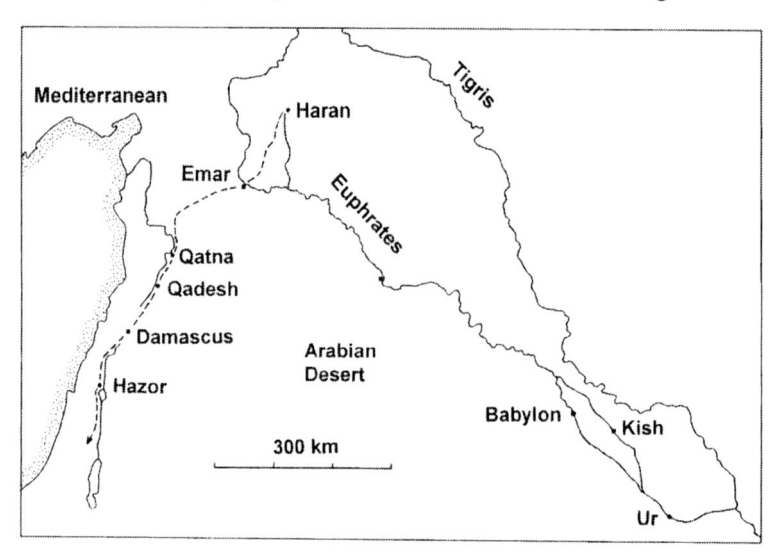

Figure 50. Map showing Abram's migration route from Ur to Haran up the River Euphrates, and from there to the Promised Land (dashed line).

What was Abram to do? Should he join his father in deserting the land of Sumer that had taught him so much? Should he abandon his reverence for the god En-lil, about whom the old priest had taught him all those years ago? On the other hand, if he stayed in Ur, with its growing food shortages, he might die of illness, starvation or war. Abram was at a major cross-roads in his life, and there was no wise old priest to guide him.

Abram went to the family shrine that his father had built at great expense onto the back of the house. The shrine was like a room of the house, but open to the clear sky above. In the centre of the end wall was a small altar with a hearth for burning incense, from which a small chimney led up the wall behind. On the left side of the altar was an offering table made of plastered bricks. The plaster was cast in the form of panelled wood, as a small copy of the great offering table in the temple of the Moon-god.

In front of the altar stood the family gods, represented by small clay figurines a few inches high. Terah would present his petitions to the family gods, in the belief that they would intercede for him before the great god, Sin.

Figure 51. Remains of a household shrine at Ur from around the time of Abraham, as excavated by Leonard Woolley.

Abram did not believe in Sin, or in the family gods that were supposed to introduce the worshipper to the great god. The old priest had explained to Abram when he was young that there was only one Holy Trinity: Anu, En-lil and Enki... and that the astral trinity of sun, moon and morning star were just created things, not gods.

Nevertheless, Abram liked to go into the family shrine at night. Not when the moon was full, when his father was bowing down and worshipping it, but on the days when there was no moon and the darkness was complete. The incense smouldered with a dull red glow on the altar, and the walls of the shrine kept out the small lights from other houses, so that Abram could look up at the night sky in all its splendour. Thousands upon thousands of stars, speaking of the majesty of the God of Heaven who was enthroned above the sky.

Then Abram prayed, "En-lil, Lord Spirit, can you hear me? What is your purpose for my life?"

He sat through the night for hours, but there was no reply. Finally he fell into a deep and nightmarish sleep, full of foreboding about the future. He was dreaming of wandering, lost, on the great northern steppes that his father had told him about, but which to Abram were a foreign land. Abram's home was the land of the plain, the land of cities and gardens that appeared to be crumbling around him.

In the darkness of Abram's dream, a glowing cloud began to appear, at first amorphous in shape, and then taking the form of a man; but Abram could not see his face because it was both shining and also indistinct at the same time. Abram's subconscious mind went back to the stories that the old priest had told him about the glowing cloud that used to appear long ago in the Holy of Holies in the temple of En-lil.

"Who are you Lord?" Abram asked, not awake, but now somehow conscious of the vision before him.

"I am the LORD, Spirit of God. You must go from this

country, this people, and this house, to the land that I will show you. Your descendants will be as many as the stars of the sky, and they will be my people, and I will be their God. And through you, all the peoples of the earth shall be blessed."

So Abram obeyed the Lord, and after his father had died in Haran, he set off for the land that God had shown to him. And after Abram had arrived in the new land, God appeared to him again and showed him that he was now God's chosen priest, who would make his own sacrificial offerings to the Lord.

So Abram worshipped God in the land of Canaan, and God made a new covenant with him, saying, "I am El-shaddai (the Lord who is all sufficient).[10] Now you must continue to trust in me and walk with me in righteousness. And I will make you the father of many nations. Therefore, you will no longer be called Abram (exalted father), but Abraham (father of a multitude), because the breath of El is in you to make you the father of many nations...

---

[10] The prefix 'El' in the Semitic tongue is equivalent to 'En' in Sumerian, meaning Lord.

Epilogue

More than 500 years after God appeared to Abraham, he revealed himself to Moses in the Burning Bush (Exodus 3:14). In that encounter, God also revealed his new name 'YHWH' (Yahweh). However, this name was not placed into its full historical context until after Moses' first contest with the magicians of Pharaoh. Then God appeared to Moses again and announced (Exodus 6:3):

> *"I appeared to Abraham, to Isaac and to Jacob as El Shaddai, but by my name YHWH I did not make myself known to them."*

But this claim that Abraham did not know the name of Yahweh is a major problem for the interpretation of Genesis, because God is frequently referred to in Genesis by the name Yahweh, both in narrative and dialogue.

This problem has led most scholars to presume that Genesis was composed long after the events that it describes, by which time the divine name Yahweh was in common use. However, this raises the question of the source of the Mesopotamian material in Genesis, such as the Flood Story.

To explain this material, many scholars have inferred that Genesis was composed long after the monarchy of David and Solomon, during the time when the Israelites were exiled to Babylon, after the destruction of Jerusalem in 586 BC.

This theory, pioneered in the late nineteenth century by the German theologian Julius Wellhausen, proposed that Genesis was written as a kind of 'invented history' to help the people to come to terms with their exile from Israel and the destruction of their temple in Jerusalem.

However, in 1936, Percy (P. J.) Wiseman offered a radical alternative solution to the problem of Exodus 6:3, claiming that Genesis was largely written in cuneiform by the Patriarchs but was transcribed and compiled (i.e. edited) by Moses. Wiseman suggested that during the transcription, Moses replaced an earlier divine name with that of Yahweh.

Wiseman speculated that the divine name used in the old cuneiform sources was El Shaddai. However, I suggested in the previous chapter that the name El Shaddai, which was a new revelation to Abraham, was a development of the older divine name El-lil (En-lil in Sumerian), 'The Lord, Breath [of God]' which Abraham had known in Mesopotamia.

If we want to know what form of divine name was most commonly used by Abraham and his family, we use a technique often employed by scholars, which is to see which divine names are incorporated into the 'given names' of places or children.

When we examine the Genesis account, we do not see any names based on Yahweh, the name by which God revealed himself to Moses. However, we do see several names based on 'El' (Lord). Examples are: Ishma-el (The Lord hears, Gen 16:11); Beth-el (The House of the Lord, Gen 28:19); Isra-el (He struggles with the Lord, Gen 32:28) and Peni-el (Face of the Lord, Gen 32:30). We even see the double and triple use of El in two instances: El Beth-el (The Lord of the House of the Lord, Gen 35:7) and El El-ohe Isra-el (The Lord, the Lord of him who struggles with the Lord, Gen 33:20). Finally, we note that the descendants of Jacob adopted this very name of God as the name of their nation: Isra-el.

Supposing that Moses received a document that used El as

the name for God, what is the evidence that this document may have been written in cuneiform?

The answer comes from the 'Amarna Letters', which are a set of correspondence between Egyptian Pharaohs and their Canaanite vassals, written around 1500 BC. These letters were written in Akkadian (Semitic) cuneiform on clay tablets, indicating that Akkadian was the principle language of diplomatic communication at the time, even in Egypt. Therefore, if Moses received any written records about the early history of the patriarchs in Mesopotamia, these were probably written in Akkadian.

We are told in Acts 7:22 that 'Moses was educated in all the wisdom of the Egyptians.' Therefore, we can be confident that Moses was able to read any documents handed down to him in Akkadian cuneiform. But this raises the question of who might have written such a record in the first place.

There is no indication in Genesis that Abraham acquired already written accounts from Mesopotamia, or that he wrote any such accounts himself. The nomadic way of life that Abraham adopted did not lend itself to the very specialised academic study that was necessary to become a scribe of cuneiform.

However, Abraham's great grandson, Joseph, held an administrative position that required such knowledge. Since Joseph oversaw the government of all Egypt, including the keeping of meticulous records of food distribution, it is almost inevitable that he must have learned to read and write cuneiform. Therefore, it seems likely that Joseph first committed into writing the oral accounts passed down to him through Abraham.

Returning to the question of the use of divine names in Genesis, we can conclude from the above argument that if Moses edited the written account of Genesis, he used the new name Yahweh to replace the older divine name El. Appropriately, the most common translation of Yahweh in English ('the LORD') is also an accurate translation of El.

However, this leaves us with one critical question. Why did Moses feel obliged to replace the older divine name at all?

To answer this question we have to examine the account of Genesis from the point of view of the Canaanites.

The Canaanites were the original inhabitants of the Promised Land, and they had also once worshipped El as the supreme God. Like Abraham, the Canaanites had learned of the God El from Mesopotamia, but by the time of Moses, the Canaanites had debased the name of El and had made Baal the supreme God in his place. Because of this, the name of El lost its distinctiveness, so that by the time of Moses its plural form (elohim) had become a generic word for any god. Therefore, it was to combat this debasing of the name of El that the new name of Yahweh was revealed to Moses.

History has a way of repeating itself, so perhaps it is not surprising that something very similar had occurred 2000 years before the time of Moses, in ancient Mesopotamia. In those far-off days, when the great city of Uruk was at its zenith, the God of Heaven was recognised as the supreme God, and his name (An) was represented in cuneiform by an eight pointed star. But the priests of Uruk elevated the goddess Ishtar to the position of the Queen of Heaven, so that she usurped the place of the God of Heaven. Then the God of Heaven was relegated to the position of a remote and ineffectual deity, and the sign of the star became a generic word for any god.

It was this twice-repeated process of debasement of the name of God that probably caused Moses to replace those names when he transcribed the ancient cuneiform records into the Book of Genesis. He replaced the star sign by the Hebrew *elohim* (which we translate as 'God'), and he replaced the name of El by the Hebrew *Yahweh* (which we translate as 'LORD').

This leaves us with the most difficult question, concerning the origin of the name *Yahweh elohim*, which is used uniquely in Genesis Chapter 2. Perhaps this was used to replace the signs

'En-ki' (literally 'Lord of the Earth' in Sumerian).

It was necessary that the Sumerian names for the gods of the Trinity be replaced by the new name of Yahweh in order to demonstrate clearly that all these divine persons are one and the same God. Thus, the revelation to Moses emphasised God's oneness, in order to counteract the corruption of the Sumerians, who had turned the Trinity into the beginnings of a pantheon of gods.

The final third of Genesis (Ch 37-50), which describes the story of Joseph in Egypt, has a different pattern in the use of divine names. Unlike the earlier chapters of Genesis, where Elohim and Yahweh are used with almost equal frequency in both narrative in dialogue, the Joseph story almost exclusively uses Elohim in dialogue and Yahweh in narrative. This story cannot have been written by Joseph because it describes his own death. Therefore, it was probably passed down orally by Joseph's descendants in Egypt.

Joseph's descendants did not know the name of Yahweh. Therefore, in dialogue (human speech) they exclusively referred to God by the name Elohim. When Moses came to write the story down, he preserved this usage when he quoted human speech. However, when he wrote the narrative, he used the new name for God that had first been revealed to him. So the distribution of divine names in Genesis highlights the distinction between the early transcribed account of Joseph and the later written account of Moses.

Further evidence for this process comes from the observation by Duane Garrett that the story of Joseph (written by Moses) appears to have been inserted into an earlier structure of the book of Genesis. This structure generally consists of alternating genealogies and stories. The genealogies are used to tie the stories together and they give the book its Greek name, 'Genesis'.

The stories of Adam, Noah and Abraham, which stretch from the beginning to the end of the Mesopotamian period of

Genesis, are linked together by two schematic genealogies, each of ten generations, which were probably compiled long after the stories that they join.

The period spanned by these genealogies stretches from about 6000 BC to 2000 BC, equal in length to the whole of subsequent human history. However, the short summary given in the first twelve books of Genesis is enough to interpret the detailed archaeological and historical record from Mesopotamia, so that at last we can begin to understand the origins of our culture and our faith.

Appendix

Summary of major periods
and excavation levels

C-14 age B.C.	Name of Period in Mesopotamia		General name of Period
540			
	Neo Babylonian Empire		
630			
	Neo Assyrian Empire		Iron age
930			
1200	Second Assyrian Empire First Babylonian Empire First Assyrian Empire		
			Late Bronze
	Kassites		
1600			
	Old Babylonian Period	Babylon Larsa Isin	Middle Bronze
2020			
2200	3rd Dynasty of Ur Gutian period Akkadian Dynasty		
2370			
2600	Early	III	
	Dynastic II		Early Bronze
2750	Period		
		I	
3000			
3200	Proto-literate (Jemdet Nasr)		
		Late	
3600	Uruk		Chalcolithic
		Early	
4000			
		Late	
4500	Ubaid		
		Early	
5400			Neolithic
		Late	
5700	Halaf		
		Early	
6100			

(In some nomenclature, the Ubaid period overlaps with Halaf)

Yr BC	Period	Eridu	Uruk	Typical pottery
3000	Early Dynastic I		1	
	Proto-literate (Jemdet Nasr)		2, 3a, 3b, 3c	
3300		1	4a	
	Late Uruk	2	4b, 5	
3600			6, 7	
		3	8, 9	
	Early Uruk	4	10, 11, 12, 13	
		5	14	
4000			15	
		6	16	----Ur Flood layer----
	Late Ubaid	7	17	
		8	18	
	Early Ubaid	9, 10, 11, 12		
	Eridu 2	13, 14		
5000?	Eridu 1	15, 16, 17, 18, 19		

Sources

The principle sources of information for this book are given in the reference list below. For references with two quoted dates, the first represents the earliest edition (sometimes in a foreign language). The later date represents the edition for which page numbers are given.

Alster, B. (1976). On the earliest Sumerian literary tradition. *J. Cuneiform Studies* **28**, 109-126.

Biggs, R. D. (1966). The Abu Salabikh tablets. *J. Cuneiform Studies* **20**, 73-88.

Braaten, L. J. (2001). The voice of Wisdom: a creation context for the emergence of Trinitarian language. *Wesleyan Theological J.* **36**, 31-56.

Burney, C. (1977). *From Village to Empire/The Ancient Near East*. Phaidon/Univ. Cornell Press, 224 p.

Clifford, R. J. (1972). *The Cosmic Mountain in Canaan and the Old Testament*. Harvard Univ. Press, 221 p.

Clifford, R. J. (1994). *Creation Accounts in the Ancient Near East and in the Bible*. Catholic Biblical Quarterly Monograph Series, no. **26**, 217 p.

Cooper, J. S. (1983). *The Curse of Agade*. Johns Hopkins Univ. Press, 292 p.

Dalley, S. (1989/1991). *Myths from Mesopotamia: Creation, The Flood, Gilgamesh, and Others*. Oxford Univ. Press, 337 p.

Dickin, A. (2002). *Pagan Trinity—Holy Trinity: The Legacy of the Sumerians in Western Civilization*. Hamilton Books.127p

Finegan, J. (1979). *Archaeological History of the Ancient Middle East*. Westview Press, 456 p.

Frankfort, H. (1933). Gods and myths on Sargonid seals. *Iraq* **1**, 2-30.

Garrett, D. A. (1991). *Rethinking Genesis: the Sources and Authorship of the First Book of the Bible*. Baker Book House. 311 p.

Gibson, M. (1992). Patterns of occupation at Nippur. In: deJong Ellis, M. (Ed.), *Nippur at the Centennial*. University Museum, Philadelphia, pp. 33-54.

Green, M. W. and Nissen, H. J. (1987). Zeichenliste der archaischen texte aus Uruk, *Archaische Texte aus Uruk Band 2*. Gebr. Mann Verlag,

Hallo, W. W. (1970). Antediluvian cities. *J. Cuneiform Studies* **23**, 57-67.

Hallo, W. W. and Simpson, W. K. (1971/1998). *The Ancient Near East: A History*. Harcourt Brace College Pub., 324 p.

Hamlin, E. J. (1954). The meaning of "mountains and hills" in Isa. 41:14-16. *J. Near East Studies* **13**, 185-190.

Hassan, F. A. and Robinson, S. W. (1987). High-precision radiocarbon chronometry of ancient Egypt, and comparisons with Nubia, Palestine and Mesopotamia. *Antiquity* **61**, 119-135.

Herodotus. (Translated, Aubrey de Selincourt, 1954), *The Histories*. Penguin Books.

Hilprecht, H. V. (1903). *Explorations in Bible Lands*. A. J. Holman. 810 p.

Howard-Carter, T. (1981). The tangible evidence for the earliest Dilmun. *J. Cuneiform Studies* **33**, 210-223.

Jacobsen, T. (1939/1966). The Sumerian King List. *Assyriological Studies* **11**, Univ. Chicago Press, 216 p.

Jacobsen, T. (1976). *The Treasures of Darkness: A History of Mesopotamian Religion*. Yale Univ. Press, 273p.

Jacobsen, T. (1981). The Eridu Genesis. *J. Biblical Literature* **100**, 513-529.

Jacobsen, T. (1987). *The Harps That Once...* Yale Univ. Press, 498p.

Jastrow, M. (1915). The Civilization of Babylonia and Assyria. J.B. Lippincott, 515 p.

Keller, W. (1963/1964). *The Bible as History in Pictures*. Hodder and Stoughton, 360 p.

Kramer, S. N. (1944/1972). *Sumerian Mythology: A Study of Spiritual and Literary Achievement in the Third Millennium B. C.* Univ. Pennsylvania Press, 130 p.

Kramer, S. N. (1956/1981). *History Begins at Sumer*. Univ. Pennsylvania Press, 388 p.

Kramer, S. N. (1963/1970). *The Sumerians: Their History, Culture, and Character*. Univ. Chicago Press, 355 p.

Kramer, S. N. (1968). The Babel of tongues: a Sumerian version. *J. American Oriental Soc.* **88** (Speiser volume), 108-111.

Kramer, S. N. (1979). *From the Poetry of Sumer*. Univ. California Press, 104 p.

Kramer, S. N. and Maier, J. (1989). *Myths of Enki, The Crafty God*. Oxford Univ. Press. 272 p.

Lamberg-Karlovsky, C. C. (1982). Dilmun: gateway to immortality. *J. Near Eastern Studies* **41**, 45-50.

Lambert, W. G. (1992). Nippur in ancient ideology. In: deJong Ellis, M. (Ed.), *Nippur at the Centennial*. University Museum, Philadelphia, pp. 119-126.

Laurin, R. B. (1978). The tower of Babel revisited. In: Tuttle, G. A. (Ed.), *Biblical and Near Eastern Studies: Essays in Honor of William Sanford LaSor*. W. B. Erdmans, pp. 142-5.

Layard, A. H. (1849). *Nineveh and its Remains*. John Murray, 399 p.

Leick, G. (2001/2002). *Mesopotamia: The Invention of the City*. Penguin Books, 360 p.

Lloyd, S. (1947/1980). *Foundations in the Dust*. Thames and Hudson, 216 p.

Lloyd, S. (1978/1984). *The Archaeology of Mesopotamia: From the Old Stone Age to the Persian Conquest*. Thames and Hutton, 251 p.

Nissen, H. J. (1983/1988).*The Early History of the Ancient Near East (9000 - 2000 B.C.)*. Translated: Lutzeier, E. and Northcott, K. J. Univ. Chicago Press, 215 p.

Nissen, H. J., Damerow, P. and Englund, R. K. (1993). *Archaic Bookkeeping*. Univ. Chicago Press. 169 p.

Noldecke, A. (1936). *Uruk Vorbericht 7*.

Otto, R. (1923/1958), Harvey, J. W., Translator. *The Idea of the Holy*. Oxford Univ. Press, 232 p.

Poebel, A. (1914). *Historical and Grammatical Texts*. Pub. Babylonian Section, v. 4 & 5, Univ. Museum, Philadelphia.

Pope, M. (1975). *The Story of Archaeological Decipherment*. Thames and Hudson, 216 p.

Postgate, J. N. (1992/1994). *Early Mesopotamia: Society and Economy at the Dawn of History*. Routledge, 367 p.

Rawlinson, H. C. and Norris, E. (1861). *A Selection from the Historical Inscriptions of Chaldaea, Assyria, & Babylonia*. British Museum.

Reade, J. (2001). Assyrian king-lists, the royal tombs of Ur, and Indus origins. *J. Near Eastern Studies* **60**, 1-29.

Roaf, M. (1990). *Cultural Atlas of Mesopotamia and the Ancient Near East*. Facts on File, 238 p.

Roux, G. (1992/2001) Did the Sumerians emerge from the sea? In: *Everyday Life in Ancient Mesopotamia*. Bottero, J. (Ed.), Nevill, A. (Trans.), Edinburgh Univ. Press, pp. 3-23.

Rowton, M. B. (1960). The date of the Sumerian King List. *J. Near Eastern Studies* **19**, 156-162.

Safar, F., Mustafa, M. A. and Lloyd, S. (1981). *Eridu*. Baghdad.

Saggs, H. W. F. (1995/2000). *Peoples of the Past: Babylonians*. British Museum/Univ. Okalahoma Press, 192 p.

Schmandt-Besserat, D. (1992). *Before Writing*. Univ. Texas Press.

Seely, P. H. (1991). The firmament and the water above. Part I: The meaning of *raqia* in Gen 1:6-8. *Westminster Theological J.* **53**, 227-240.

Seely, P. H. (1992). The firmament and the water above. Part II: The meaning of 'the water above the firmament' in Gen 1:6-8. *Westminster Theological J.* **54**, 31-46.

Seely, P. H. (1997). The geographical meaning of "earth" and "seas" in Genesis 1:10. *Westminster Theological J.* **59**, 231-255.

Sollberger, E. (1962). The Tummal Inscription. *J. Cuneiform Studies* **16**, 40-47.

Van Buren, E. D. (1944). The Sacred Marriage in early times in Mesopotamia. *Orientalia* **13**, 1-72.

Van der Toorn, K. (1996). *Family Religion in Babylonia, Syria and Israel.* E. J. Brill, 491 p.

Van Dijk, J. (1964-65). Le motif cosmique dans la pensée Sumerienne. *Acta Orientalia* **28**, 1-59.

Vanstiphout, H. L. J. (1992). Repetition and Structure in the Aratta cycle: their relevance for the orality debate. In: Vogelzang, M. E. and Vanstiphout, H. L. J. (Eds), *Mesopotamian Epic Literature: Oral or Aural?* Edwin Mellen Press, 320 p.

Wenham, G. J. (1978). The coherence of the flood narrative. *Vetus Testamentum* **28**, 336-348.

Wiseman, P. J. (1936/1977). *New discoveries in Babylonia about Genesis.* In: Wiseman, D. J. (Ed.), *Clues to Creation in Genesis*, Marshall, Morgan and Scott, 232 p.

Wiseman, P. J. (1948/1977). *Creation Revealed in Six Days.* In: Wiseman, D. J. (Ed.), *Clues to Creation in Genesis*, Marshall, Morgan and Scott, 232 p.

Woolley, C. L. (1936). *Abraham: Recent Discoveries and Hebrew Origins.* Faber and Faber Ltd. 299 p.

Woolley, C. L. (1954/1963). *Excavations at Ur.* Ernest Benn, Ltd, 256 p.